A Joy For Ever
(And Its Price in the Market)

John Ruskin

Contents

A JOY FOR EVER
(AND ITS PRICE IN THE MARKET)

BY

John Ruskin

PREFACE
TO THE RE-ISSUE OF 1880.

The title of this book,--or, more accurately, of its subject;--for no author was ever less likely than I have lately become, to hope for perennial pleasure to his readers from what has cost himself the most pains,--will be, perhaps, recognised by some as the last clause of the line chosen from Keats by the good folks of Manchester, to be written in letters of gold on the cornice, or Holy rood, of the great Exhibition which inaugurated the career of so many,--since organized, by both foreign governments and our own, to encourage the production of works of art, which the producing nations, so far from intending to be their "joy for ever," only hope to sell as soon as possible. Yet the motto was chosen with uncomprehended felicity: for there never was, nor can be, any essential beauty possessed by a work of art, which is not based on the conception of its honoured permanence, and local influence, as a part of appointed and precious furniture, either in the cathedral, the house, or the joyful thoroughfare, of nations which enter their gates with thanksgiving, and their courts with praise.

"Their" courts--or "His" courts;--in the mind of such races, the expressions are synonymous: and the habits of life which recognise the delightfulness, confess also the sacredness, of homes nested round the seat of a worship unshaken by insolent theory: themselves founded on an abiding affection for the past, and care for the future; and approached by paths open only to the activities of honesty, and traversed only by the footsteps of peace.

The exposition of these truths, to which I have given the chief energy of my life, will be found in the following pages first undertaken systematically and in logical sequence; and what I have since written on the political influence of the Arts has been little more than the expansion of these first lectures, in the reprint of which not a sentence is omitted or changed.

The supplementary papers added contain, in briefest form, the aphorisms respecting principles of art-teaching of which the attention I gave to this subject during the continuance of my Professorship at Oxford confirms me in the earnest and contented re-assertion.

JOHN RUSKIN,
BRANTWOOD,
April 29th, 1880.

PREFACE
TO THE 1857 EDITION.

The greater part of the following treatise remains in the exact form in which it was read at Manchester; but the more familiar passages of it, which were trusted to extempore delivery, have been written with greater explicitness and fulness than I could give them in speaking; and a considerable number of notes are added, to explain the points which could not be sufficiently considered in the time I had at my disposal in the lecture room.

Some apology may be thought due to the reader, for an endeavour to engage his attention on a subject of which no profound study seems compatible with the work in which I am usually employed. But profound study is not, in this case, necessary either to writer or readers, while accurate study, up to a certain point, is necessary for us all. Political economy means, in plain English, nothing more than "citizen's economy"; and its first principles ought, therefore, to be understood by all who mean to take the responsibility of citizens, as those of household economy by all who take the responsibility of householders. Nor are its first principles in the least obscure: they are, many of them, disagreeable in their practical requirements, and people in general pretend that they cannot understand, because they are unwilling to obey them: or rather, by habitual disobedience, destroy their capacity of understanding them. But there is not one of the really great principles of the science which is either obscure or disputable,--which might not be taught to a youth as soon as he can be trusted with an annual allowance, or to a young lady as soon as she is of age to be taken into counsel by the housekeeper.

I might, with more appearance of justice, be blamed for thinking it necessary to enforce what everybody is supposed to know. But this fault will hardly be found with me, while the commercial events recorded daily in our journals, and still more the explanations attempted to be given of them, show that a large number of our so-called merchants are as ignorant of the nature of money as they are reckless, unjust, and unfortunate in its employment.

The statements of economical principles given in the text, though I know that most, if not all, of them are accepted by existing authorities on the science, are not supported by references, because I have never read any author on political economy, except Adam Smith, twenty years ago. Whenever I have taken up any modern book upon this subject, I have usually found it encumbered with inquiries into accidental or minor commercial results, for the pursuit of which an ordinary reader could have no leisure, and by the complication of which, it seemed to me, the authors themselves had been not unfrequently prevented from seeing to the root of the business.

Finally, if the reader should feel induced to blame me for too sanguine a statement of future possibilities in political practice, let him consider how absurd it would have appeared in the days of Edward I. if the present state of social economy had been then predicted as necessary, or even described as possible. And I believe the advance from the days of Edward I. to our own, great as it is confessedly, consists, not so much in what we have actually accomplished, as in what we are now enabled to conceive.

LECTURE I.
THE DISCOVERY AND APPLICATION OF ART.

A Lecture delivered at Manchester, July 10, 1857.

1. Among the various characteristics of the age in which we live, as compared with other ages of this not yet *very* experienced world, one of the most notable appears to me to be the just and wholesome contempt in which we hold poverty.

I repeat, the ***just*** and ***wholesome*** contempt; though I see that some of my hearers look surprised at the expression. I assure them, I use it in sincerity; and I should not have ventured to ask you to listen to me this evening, unless I had entertained a profound respect for wealth--true wealth, that is to say; for, of course, we ought to respect neither wealth nor anything else that is false of its kind: and the distinction between real and false wealth is one of the points on which I shall have a few words presently to say to you. But true wealth I hold, as I said, in great honour; and sympathize, for the most part, with that extraordinary feeling of the present age which publicly pays this honour to riches.

2. I cannot, however, help noticing how extraordinary it is, and how this epoch of ours differs from all bygone epochs in having no philosophical nor religious worshippers of the ragged godship of poverty. In the classical ages, not only were there people who voluntarily lived in tubs, and who used gravely to maintain the superiority of tub-life to town-life, but the Greeks and Latins seem to have looked on these eccentric, and I do not scruple to say, absurd people, with as much respect as we do upon large capitalists and landed proprietors; so that really, in those days, no one could be described as purse proud, but only as empty-purse proud. And no less distinct than the honour which those curious Greek people pay to their conceited poor, is the disrespectful manner in which they speak of the rich; so that one cannot listen long either to them, or to the Roman writers who imitated them, without finding oneself entangled in all sorts of plausible absurdities; hard upon being convinced of the uselessness of collecting that heavy yellow substance which we call gold, and led generally to doubt all the most established maxims of political economy.

3. Nor are matters much better in the Middle Ages. For the Greeks and Romans contented themselves with mocking at rich people, and constructing merry dialogues between Charon and Diogenes or Menippus, in which the ferryman and the cynic rejoiced together as they saw kings and rich men coming down to the shore of Acheron, in lamenting and lamentable crowds, casting their crowns into the dark waters, and searching, sometimes in vain, for the last coin out of all their treasures that could ever be of use to them.

4. But these Pagan views of the matter were indulgent, compared with those which were held in the Middle Ages, when wealth seems to have been looked upon

by the best men not only as contemptible, but as criminal. The purse round the neck is, then, one of the principal signs of condemnation in the pictured Inferno; and the Spirit of Poverty is reverenced with subjection of heart, and faithfulness of affection, like that of a loyal knight for his lady, or a loyal subject for his queen. And truly, it requires some boldness to quit ourselves of these feelings, and to confess their partiality or their error, which, nevertheless, we are certainly bound to do. For wealth is simply one of the greatest powers which can be entrusted to human hands: a power, not indeed to be envied, because it seldom makes us happy; but still less to be abdicated or despised; while, in these days, and in this country, it has become a power all the more notable, in that the possessions of a rich man are not represented, as they used to be, by wedges of gold or coffers of jewels, but by masses of men variously employed, over whose bodies and minds the wealth, according to its direction, exercises harmful or helpful influence, and becomes, in that alternative, Mammon either of Unrighteousness or of Righteousness.

5. Now, it seemed to me that since, in the name you have given to this great gathering of British pictures, you recognize them as Treasures--that is, I suppose, as part and parcel of the real wealth of the country--you might not be uninterested in tracing certain commercial questions connected with this particular form of wealth. Most persons express themselves as surprised at its quantity; not having known before to what an extent good art had been accumulated in England: and it will, therefore, I should think, be held a worthy subject of consideration, what are the political interests involved in such accumulations, what kind of labour they represent, and how this labour may in general be applied and economized, so as to produce the richest results.

6. Now, you must have patience with me, if in approaching the specialty of this subject, I dwell a little on certain points of general political science already known or established: for though thus, as I believe, established, some which I shall have occasion to rest arguments on are not yet by any means universally accepted; and therefore, though I will not lose time in any detailed defence of them, it is necessary that I should distinctly tell you in what form I receive, and wish to argue from them; and this the more, because there may perhaps be a part of my audience who have not interested themselves in political economy, as it bears on ordinary fields of labour, but may yet wish to hear in what way its principles can be applied to Art. I

shall, therefore, take leave to trespass on your patience with a few elementary statements in the outset, and with the expression of some general principles, here and
there, in the course of our particular inquiry.

7. To begin, then, with one of these necessary truisms: all economy, whether of
states, households, or individuals, may be defined to be the art of managing labour.
The world is so regulated by the laws of Providence, that a man's labour, well applied, is always amply sufficient to provide him during his life with all things needful to him, and not only with those, but with many pleasant objects of luxury; and
yet farther, to procure him large intervals of healthful rest and serviceable leisure.
And a nation's labour, well applied, is, in like manner, amply sufficient to provide
its whole population with good food and comfortable habitation; and not with those
only, but with good education besides, and objects of luxury, art treasures, such as
these you have around you now. But by those same laws of Nature and Providence,
if the labour of the nation or of the individual be misapplied, and much more if it
be insufficient,--if the nation or man be indolent and unwise,--suffering and want
result, exactly in proportion to the indolence and improvidence--to the refusal of
labour, or to the misapplication of it. Wherever you see want, or misery, or degradation, in this world about you, there, be sure, either industry has been wanting, or
industry has been in error. It is not accident, it is not Heaven-commanded calamity,
it is not the original and inevitable evil of man's nature, which fill your streets with
lamentation, and your graves with prey. It is only that, when there should have
been providence, there has been waste; when there should have been labour, there
has been lasciviousness; and wilfulness, when there should have been subordina-
tion.[1]

> [Note 1: Proverbs xiii. 23: "Much food is in the tillage of the poor, but there
> is that is destroyed for want of judgment."]

8. Now, we have warped the word "economy" in our English language into a
meaning which it has no business whatever to bear. In our use of it, it constantly
signifies merely sparing or saving; economy of money means saving money--econo-
my of time, sparing time, and so on. But that is a wholly barbarous use of the word-
-barbarous in a double sense, for it is not English, and it is bad Greek; barbarous in
a treble sense, for it is not English, it is bad Greek, and it is worse sense. Economy
no more means saving money than it means spending money. It means, the admin-

istration of a house; its stewardship; spending or saving, that is, whether money or time, or anything else, to the best possible advantage. In the simplest and clearest definition of it, economy, whether public or private, means the wise management of labour; and it means this mainly in three senses: namely, first, ***applying*** your labour rationally; secondly, ***preserving*** its produce carefully; lastly, ***distributing*** its produce seasonably.

9. I say first, applying your labour rationally; that is, so as to obtain the most precious things you can, and the most lasting things, by it: not growing oats in land where you can grow wheat, nor putting fine embroidery on a stuff that will not wear. Secondly, preserving its produce carefully; that is to say, laying up your wheat wisely in storehouses for the time of famine, and keeping your embroidery watchfully from the moth: and lastly, distributing its produce seasonably; that is to say, being able to carry your corn at once to the place where the people are hungry, and your embroideries to the places where they are gay; so fulfilling in all ways the Wise Man's description, whether of the queenly housewife or queenly nation: "She riseth while it is yet night, and giveth meat to her household, and a portion to her maidens. She maketh herself coverings of tapestry, her clothing is silk and purple. Strength and honour are in her clothing, and she shall rejoice in time to come."

10. Now, you will observe that in this description of the perfect economist, or mistress of a household, there is a studied expression of the balanced division of her care between the two great objects of utility and splendour: in her right hand, food and flax, for life and clothing; in her left hand, the purple and the needlework, for honour and for beauty. All perfect housewifery or national economy is known by these two divisions; wherever either is wanting, the economy is imperfect. If the motive of pomp prevails, and the care of the national economist is directed only to the accumulation of gold, and of pictures, and of silk and marble, you know at once that the time must soon come when all these treasures shall be scattered and blasted in national ruin. If, on the contrary, the element of utility prevails, and the nation disdains to occupy itself in any wise with the arts of beauty or delight, not only a certain quantity of its energy calculated for exercise in those arts alone must be entirely wasted, which is bad economy, but also the passions connected with the utilities of property become morbidly strong, and a mean lust of accumulation merely for the sake of accumulation, or even of labour merely for the sake of labour, will

banish at last the serenity and the morality of life, as completely, and perhaps more ignobly, than even the lavishness of pride, and the likeness of pleasure. And similarly, and much more visibly, in private and household economy, you may judge always of its perfectness by its fair balance between the use and the pleasure of its possessions. You will see the wise cottager's garden trimly divided between its well-set vegetables, and its fragrant flowers; you will see the good housewife taking pride in her pretty table-cloth, and her glittering shelves, no less than in her well-dressed dish, and her full storeroom; the care in her countenance will alternate with gaiety, and though you will reverence her in her seriousness, you will know her best by her smile.

11. Now, as you will have anticipated, I am going to address you, on this and our succeeding evening, chiefly on the subject of that economy which relates rather to the garden than the farm-yard. I shall ask you to consider with me the kind of laws by which we shall best distribute the beds of our national garden, and raise in it the sweetest succession of trees pleasant to the sight, and (in no forbidden sense) to be desired to make us wise. But, before proceeding to open this specialty of our subject, let me pause for a few moments to plead with you for the acceptance of that principle of government or authority which must be at the root of all economy, whether for use or for pleasure. I said, a few minutes ago, that a nation's labour, well applied, was amply sufficient to provide its whole population with good food, comfortable clothing, and pleasant luxury. But the good, instant, and constant application is everything. We must not, when our strong hands are thrown out of work, look wildly about for want of something to do with them. If ever we feel that want, it is a sign that all our household is out of order. Fancy a farmer's wife, to whom one or two of her servants should come at twelve o'clock at noon, crying that they had got nothing to do; that they did not know what to do next: and fancy still farther, the said farmer's wife looking hopelessly about her rooms and yard, they being all the while considerably in disorder, not knowing where to set the spare handmaidens to work, and at last complaining bitterly that she had been obliged to give them their dinner for nothing. That's the type of the kind of political economy we practise too often in England. Would you not at once assert of such a mistress that she knew nothing of her duties? and would you not be certain, if the household were rightly managed, the mistress would be only too glad at any moment to have the

help of any number of spare hands; that she would know in an instant what to set them to;--in an instant what part of to-morrow's work might be most serviceably forwarded, what part of next month's work most wisely provided for, or what new task of some profitable kind undertaken; and when the evening came, and she dismissed her servants to their recreation or their rest, or gathered them to the reading round the work-table, under the eaves in the sunset, would you not be sure to find that none of them had been overtasked by her, just because none had been left idle; that everything had been accomplished because all had been employed; that the kindness of the mistress had aided her presence of mind, and the slight labour had been entrusted to the weak, and the formidable to the strong; and that as none had been dishonoured by inactivity, so none had been broken by toil?

12. Now, the precise counterpart of such a household would be seen in a nation in which political economy was rightly understood. You complain of the difficulty of finding work for your men. Depend upon it, the real difficulty rather is to find men for your work. The serious question for you is not how many you have to feed, but how much you have to do; it is our inactivity, not our hunger, that ruins us: let us never fear that our servants should have a good appetite--our wealth is in their strength, not in their starvation. Look around this island of yours, and see what you have to do in it. The sea roars against your harbourless cliffs--you have to build the breakwater, and dig the port of refuge; the unclean pestilence ravins in your streets--you have to bring the full stream from the hills, and to send the free winds through the thoroughfare; the famine blanches your lips and eats away your flesh--you have to dig the moor and dry the marsh, to bid the morass give forth instead of engulfing, and to wring the honey and oil out of the rock. These things, and thousands such, we have to do, and shall have to do constantly, on this great farm of ours; for do not suppose that it is anything else than that. Precisely the same laws of economy which apply to the cultivation of a farm or an estate, apply to the cultivation of a province or of an island. Whatever rebuke you would address to the improvident master of an ill-managed patrimony, precisely that rebuke we should address to ourselves, so far as we leave our population in idleness and our country in disorder. What would you say to the lord of an estate who complained to you of his poverty and disabilities, and when you pointed out to him that his land was half of it overrun with weeds, and that his fences were all in ruin, and that his cattle-sheds

were roofless, and his labourers lying under the hedges faint for want of food, he answered to you that it would ruin him to weed his land or to roof his sheds--that those were too costly operations for him to undertake, and that he knew not how to feed his labourers nor pay them? Would you not instantly answer, that instead of ruining him to weed his fields, it would save him; that his inactivity was his destruction, and that to set his labourers to work was to feed them? Now, you may add acre to acre, and estate to estate, as far as you like, but you will never reach a compass of ground which shall escape from the authority of these simple laws. The principles which are right in the administration of a few fields, are right also in the administration of a great country from horizon to horizon: idleness does not cease to be ruinous because it is extensive, nor labour to be productive because it is universal.

13. Nay, but you reply, there is one vast difference between the nation's economy and the private man's: the farmer has full authority over his labourers; he can direct them to do what is needed to be done, whether they like it or not; and he can turn them away if they refuse to work, or impede others in their working, or are disobedient, or quarrelsome. There *is* this great difference; it is precisely this difference on which I wish to fix your attention, for it is precisely this difference which you have to do away with. We know the necessity of authority in farm, or in fleet, or in army; but we commonly refuse to admit it in the body of the nation. Let us consider this point a little.

14. In the various awkward and unfortunate efforts which the French have made at the development of a social system, they have at least stated one true principle, that of fraternity or brotherhood. Do not be alarmed; they got all wrong in their experiments, because they quite forgot that this fact of fraternity implied another fact quite as important--that of paternity, or fatherhood. That is to say, if they were to regard the nation as one family, the condition of unity in that family consisted no less in their having a head, or a father, than in their being faithful and affectionate members, or brothers. But we must not forget this, for we have long confessed it with our lips, though we refuse to confess it in our lives. For half an hour every Sunday we expect a man in a black gown, supposed to be telling us truth, to address us as brethren, though we should be shocked at the notion of any brotherhood existing among us out of church. And we can hardly read a few sentences on

any political subject without running a chance of crossing the phrase "paternal government," though we should be utterly horror-struck at the idea of governments claiming anything like a father's authority over us. Now, I believe those two formal phrases are in both instances perfectly binding and accurate, and that the image of the farm and its servants which I have hitherto used, as expressing a wholesome national organization, fails only of doing so, not because it is too domestic, but because it is not domestic enough; because the real type of a well-organized nation must be presented, not by a farm cultivated by servants who wrought for hire, and might be turned away if they refused to labour, but by a farm in which the master was a father, and in which all the servants were sons; which implied, therefore, in all its regulations, not merely the order of expediency, but the bonds of affection and responsibilities of relationship; and in which all acts and services were not only to be sweetened by brotherly concord, but to be enforced by fatherly authority.[2]

[Note 2: See note 1st, in Addenda.]

15. Observe, I do not mean in the least that we ought to place such an authority in the hands of any one person, or of any class or body of persons. But I do mean to say that as an individual who conducts himself wisely must make laws for himself which at some time or other may appear irksome or injurious, but which, precisely at the time they appear most irksome, it is most necessary he should obey, so a nation which means to conduct itself wisely, must establish authority over itself, vested either in kings, councils, or laws, which it must resolve to obey, even at times when the law or authority appears irksome to the body of the people, or injurious to certain masses of it. And this kind of national law has hitherto been only judicial; contented, that is, with an endeavour to prevent and punish violence and crime: but, as we advance in our social knowledge, we shall endeavour to make our government paternal as well as judicial; that is, to establish such laws and authorities as may at once direct us in our occupations, protect us against our follies, and visit us in our distresses: a government which shall repress dishonesty, as now it punishes theft; which shall show how the discipline of the masses may be brought to aid the toils of peace, as discipline of the masses has hitherto knit the sinews of battle; a government which shall have its soldiers of the ploughshare as well as its soldiers of the sword, and which shall distribute more proudly its golden crosses of industry--golden as the glow of the harvest, than now it grants its bronze crosses of

honour--bronzed with the crimson of blood.

16. I have not, of course, time to insist on the nature or details of government of this kind; only I wish to plead for your several and future consideration of this one truth, that the notion of Discipline and Interference lies at the very root of all human progress or power; that the "Let-alone" principle is, in all things which man has to do with, the principle of death; that it is ruin to him, certain and total, if he lets his land alone--if he lets his fellow-men alone--if he lets his own soul alone. That his whole life, on the contrary, must, if it is healthy life, be continually one of ploughing and pruning, rebuking and helping, governing and punishing; and that therefore it is only in the concession of some great principle of restraint and interference in national action that he can ever hope to find the secret of protection against national degradation. I believe that the masses have a right to claim education from their government; but only so far as they acknowledge the duty of yielding obedience to their government. I believe they have a right to claim employment from their governors; but only so far as they yield to the governor the direction and discipline of their labour; and it is only so far as they grant to the men whom they may set over them the father's authority to check the childishnesses of national fancy, and direct the waywardnesses of national energy, that they have a right to ask that none of their distresses should be unrelieved, none of their weaknesses unwatched; and that no grief, nor nakedness, nor peril, should exist for them, against which the father's hand was not outstretched, or the father's shield uplifted.[3]

[Note 3: Compare Wordsworth's Essay on the Poor Law Amendment Bill. I quote one important passage: "But, if it be not safe to touch the abstract question of man's right in a social state to help himself even in the last extremity, may we not still contend for the duty of a Christian government, standing *in loco parentis* towards all its subjects, to make such effectual provision that no one shall be in danger of perishing either through the neglect or harshness of its legislation? Or, waiving this, is it not indisputable that the claim of the State to the allegiance, involves the protection of the subject? And, as all rights in one party impose a correlative duty upon another, it follows that the right of the State to require the services of its members, even to the jeopardizing of their lives in the common defence, establishes a right in the people (not to be gainsaid by utilitarians and economists) to public support when, from any cause, they may be unable to support themselves."--(See note 2nd, in Addenda.)]

17. Now, I have pressed this upon you at more length than is needful or proportioned to our present purposes of inquiry, because I would not for the first time speak to you on this subject of political economy without clearly stating what I believe to be its first grand principle. But its bearing on the matter in hand is chiefly to prevent you from at once too violently dissenting from me when what I may state to you as advisable economy in art appears to imply too much restraint or interference with the freedom of the patron or artist. We are a little apt, though on the whole a prudent nation, to act too immediately on our impulses, even in matters merely commercial; much more in those involving continual appeals to our fancies. How far, therefore, the proposed systems or restraints may be advisable, it is for you to judge; only I pray you not to be offended with them merely because they *are* systems and restraints.

18. Do you at all recollect that interesting passage of Carlyle, in which he compares, in this country and at this day, the understood and commercial value of man and horse; and in which he wonders that the horse, with its inferior brains and its awkward hoofiness, instead of handiness, should be always worth so many tens or scores of pounds in the market, while the man, so far from always commanding his price in the market, would often be thought to confer a service on the community by simply killing himself out of their way? Well, Carlyle does not answer his own question, because he supposes we shall at once see the answer. The value of the horse consists simply in the fact of your being able to put a bridle on him. The value of the man consists precisely in the same thing. If you can bridle him, or, which is better, if he can bridle himself, he will be a valuable creature directly. Otherwise, in a commercial point of view, his value is either nothing, or accidental only. Only, of course, the proper bridle of man is not a leathern one: what kind of texture it is rightly made of, we find from that command, "Be ye not as the horse or as the mule which have no understanding, whose mouths must be held in with bit and bridle." You are not to be without the reins, indeed; but they are to be of another kind: "I will guide thee with mine Eye." So the bridle of man is to be the Eye of God; and if he rejects that guidance, then the next best for him is the horse's and the mule's, which have no understanding; and if he rejects that, and takes the bit fairly in his teeth, then there is nothing left for him than the blood that comes out of the city,

up to the horse-bridles.

19. Quitting, however, at last these general and serious laws of government--or rather bringing them down to our own business in hand--we have to consider three points of discipline in that particular branch of human labour which is concerned, not with procuring of food, but the expression of emotion; we have to consider respecting art: first, how to apply our labour to it; then, how to accumulate or preserve the results of labour; and then, how to distribute them. But since in art the labour which we have to employ is the labour of a particular class of men--men who have special genius for the business--we have not only to consider how to apply the labour, but, first of all, how to produce the labourer; and thus the question in this particular case becomes fourfold: first, how to get your man of genius; then, how to employ your man of genius; then, how to accumulate and preserve his work in the greatest quantity; and, lastly, how to distribute his work to the best national advantage. Let us take up these questions in succession.

20. I. Discovery.--How are we to get our men of genius: that is to say, by what means may we produce among us, at any given time, the greatest quantity of effective art-intellect? A wide question, you say, involving an account of all the best means of art education. Yes, but I do not mean to go into the consideration of those; I want only to state the few principles which lie at the foundation of the matter. Of these, the first is that you have always to find your artist, not to make him; you can't manufacture him, any more than you can manufacture gold. You can find him, and refine him: you dig him out as he lies nugget-fashion in the mountain-stream; you bring him home; and you make him into current coin, or household plate, but not one grain of him can you originally produce. A certain quantity of art-intellect is born annually in every nation, greater or less according to the nature and cultivation of the nation, or race of men; but a perfectly fixed quantity annually, not increasable by one grain. You may lose it, or you may gather it; you may let it lie loose in the ravine, and buried in the sands, or you may make kings' thrones of it, and overlay temple gates with it, as you choose: but the best you can do with it is always merely sifting, melting, hammering, purifying--never creating.

21. And there is another thing notable about this artistical gold; not only is it limited in quantity, but in use. You need not make thrones or golden gates with it unless you like, but assuredly you can't do anything else with it. You can't make

knives of it, nor armour, nor railroads. The gold won't cut you, and it won't carry you: put it to a mechanical use, and you destroy it at once. It is quite true that in the greatest artists, their proper artistical faculty is united with every other; and you may make use of the other faculties, and let the artistical one lie dormant. For aught I know, there may be two or three Leonardo da Vincis employed at this moment in your harbours and railroads: but you are not employing their Leonardesque or golden faculty there,--you are only oppressing and destroying it. And the artistical gift in average men is not joined with others: your born painter, if you don't make a painter of him, won't be a first-rate merchant, or lawyer; at all events, whatever he turns out, his own special gift is unemployed by you; and in no wise helps him in that other business. So here you have a certain quantity of a particular sort of intelligence, produced for you annually by providential laws, which you can only make use of by setting it to its own proper work, and which any attempt to use otherwise involves the dead loss of so much human energy.

22. Well then, supposing we wish to employ it, how is it to be best discovered and refined? It is easily enough discovered. To wish to employ it is to discover it. All that you need is, a school of trial[4] in every important town, in which those idle farmers' lads whom their masters never can keep out of mischief, and those stupid tailors' 'prentices who are always stitching the sleeves in wrong way upwards, may have a try at this other trade; only this school of trial must not be entirely regulated by formal laws of art education, but must ultimately be the workshop of a good master painter, who will try the lads with one kind of art and another, till he finds out what they are fit for.

[Note 4: See note 3rd, in Addenda.]

23. Next, after your trial school, you want your easy and secure employment, which is the matter of chief importance. For, even on the present system, the boys who have really intense art capacity, generally make painters of themselves; but then, the best half of their early energy is lost in the battle of life. Before a good painter can get employment, his mind has always been embittered, and his genius distorted. A common mind usually stoops, in plastic chill, to whatever is asked of it, and scrapes or daubs its way complacently into public favour.[5] But your great men quarrel with you, and you revenge yourselves by starving them for the first half of their lives. Precisely in the degree in which any painter possesses original genius, is

at present the increase of moral certainty that during his early years he will have a hard battle to fight; and that just at the time when his conceptions ought to be full and happy, his temper gentle, and his hopes enthusiastic--just at that most critical period, his heart is full of anxieties and household cares; he is chilled by disappointments, and vexed by injustice; he becomes obstinate in his errors, no less than in his virtues, and the arrows of his aims are blunted, as the reeds of his trust are broken.

[Note 5: See note 4th, in Addenda.]

24. What we mainly want, therefore, is a means of sufficient and unagitated employment: not holding out great prizes for which young painters are to scramble; but furnishing all with adequate support, and opportunity to display such power as they possess without rejection or mortification. I need not say that the best field of labour of this kind would be presented by the constant progress of public works involving various decoration; and we will presently examine what kind of public works may thus, advantageously for the nation, be in constant progress. But a more important matter even than this of steady employment, is the kind of criticism with which you, the public, receive the works of the young men submitted to you. You may do much harm by indiscreet praise and by indiscreet blame; but remember the chief harm is always done by blame. It stands to reason that a young man's work cannot be perfect. It ***must*** be more or less ignorant; it must be more or less feeble; it is likely that it may be more or less experimental, and if experimental, here and there mistaken. If, therefore, you allow yourself to launch out into sudden barking at the first faults you see, the probability is that you are abusing the youth for some defect naturally and inevitably belonging to that stage of his progress; and that you might just as rationally find fault with a child for not being as prudent as a privy councillor, or with a kitten for not being as grave as a cat.

25. But there is one fault which you may be quite sure is unnecessary, and therefore a real and blamable fault: that is haste, involving negligence. Whenever you see that a young man's work is either bold or slovenly, then you may attack it firmly; sure of being right. If his work is bold, it is insolent; repress his insolence: if it is slovenly, it is indolent; spur his indolence. So long as he works in that dashing or impetuous way, the best hope for him is in your contempt: and it is only by the fact of his seeming not to seek your approbation that you may conjecture he deserves it.

26. But if he does deserve it, be sure that you give it him, else you not only run a chance of driving him from the right road by want of encouragement, but you deprive yourselves of the happiest privilege you will ever have of rewarding his labour. For it is only the young who can receive much reward from men's praise: the old, when they are great, get too far beyond and above you to care what you think of them. You may urge them then with sympathy, and surround them then with acclamation; but they will doubt your pleasure, and despise your praise. You might have cheered them in their race through the asphodel meadows of their youth; you might have brought the proud, bright scarlet into their faces, if you had but cried once to them "Well done," as they dashed up to the first goal of their early ambition. But now, their pleasure is in memory, and their ambition is in heaven. They can be kind to you, but you nevermore can be kind to them. You may be fed with the fruit and fulness of their old age, but you were as the nipping blight to them in their blossoming, and your praise is only as the warm winds of autumn to the dying branches.

27. There is one thought still, the saddest of all, bearing on this withholding of early help. It is possible, in some noble natures, that the warmth and the affections of childhood may remain unchilled, though unanswered; and that the old man's heart may still be capable of gladness, when the long-withheld sympathy is given at last. But in these noble natures it nearly always happens that the chief motive of earthly ambition has not been to give delight to themselves, but to their parents. Every noble youth looks back, as to the chiefest joy which this world's honour ever gave him, to the moment when first he saw his father's eyes flash with pride, and his mother turn away her head, lest he should take her tears for tears of sorrow. Even the lover's joy, when some worthiness of his is acknowledged before his mistress, is not so great as that, for it is not so pure--the desire to exalt himself in her eyes mixes with that of giving her delight; but he does not need to exalt himself in his parents' eyes: it is with the pure hope of giving them pleasure that he comes to tell them what he has done, or what has been said of him; and therefore he has a purer pleasure of his own. And this purest and best of rewards you keep from him if you can: you feed him in his tender youth with ashes and dishonour; and then you come to him, obsequious, but too late, with your sharp laurel crown, the dew all dried from off its leaves; and you thrust it into his languid hand, and he looks at you wistfully.

What shall he do with it? What can he do, but go and lay it on his mother's grave?

28. Thus, then, you see that you have to provide for your young men: first, the searching or discovering school; then the calm employment; then the justice of praise: one thing more you have to do for them in preparing them for full service-- namely, to make, in the noble sense of the word, gentlemen of them; that is to say, to take care that their minds receive such training, that in all they paint they shall see and feel the noblest things. I am sorry to say, that of all parts of an artist's education, this is the most neglected among us; and that even where the natural taste and feeling of the youth have been pure and true, where there was the right stuff in him to make a gentleman of, you may too frequently discern some jarring rents in his mind, and elements of degradation in his treatment of subject, owing to want of gentle training, and of the liberal influence of literature. This is quite visible in our greatest artists, even in men like Turner and Gainsborough; while in the common grade of our second-rate painters the evil attains a pitch which is far too sadly manifest to need my dwelling upon it. Now, no branch of art economy is more important than that of making the intellect at your disposal pure as well as powerful; so that it may always gather for you the sweetest and fairest things. The same quantity of labour from the same man's hand, will, according as you have trained him, produce a lovely and useful work, or a base and hurtful one; and depend upon it, whatever value it may possess, by reason of the painter's skill, its chief and final value, to any nation, depends upon its being able to exalt and refine, as well as to please; and that the picture which most truly deserves the name of an art-treasure is that which has been painted by a good man.

29. You cannot but see how far this would lead, if I were to enlarge upon it. I must take it up as a separate subject some other time: only noticing at present that no money could be better spent by a nation than in providing a liberal and disciplined education for its painters, as they advance into the critical period of their youth; and that, also, a large part of their power during life depends upon the kind of subjects which you, the public, ask them for, and therefore the kind of thoughts with which you require them to be habitually familiar. I shall have more to say on this head when we come to consider what employment they should have in public buildings.

30. There are many other points of nearly as much importance as these, to be

explained with reference to the development of genius; but I should have to ask you to come and hear six lectures instead of two if I were to go into their detail. For instance, I have not spoken of the way in which you ought to look for those artificers in various manual trades, who, without possessing the order of genius which you would desire to devote to higher purposes, yet possess wit, and humour, and sense of colour, and fancy for form--all commercially valuable as quantities of intellect, and all more or less expressible in the lower arts of iron-work, pottery, decorative sculpture, and such like. But these details, interesting as they are, I must commend to your own consideration, or leave for some future inquiry. I want just now only to set the bearings of the entire subject broadly before you, with enough of detailed illustration to make it intelligible; and therefore I must quit the first head of it here, and pass to the second--namely, how best to employ the genius we discover. A certain quantity of able hands and heads being placed at our disposal, what shall we most advisably set them upon?

31. II. APPLICATION.--There are three main points the economist has to attend to in this.

First, To set his men to various work.

Secondly, To easy work.

Thirdly, To lasting work.

I shall briefly touch on the first two, for I want to arrest your attention on the last.

32. I say first to various work. Supposing you have two men of equal power as landscape painters--and both of them have an hour at your disposal. You would not set them both to paint the same piece of landscape. You would, of course, rather have two subjects than a repetition of one.

Well, supposing them sculptors, will not the same rule hold? You naturally conclude at once that it will; but you will have hard work to convince your modern architects of that. They will put twenty men to work, to carve twenty capitals; and all shall be the same. If I could show you the architects' yards in England just now, all open at once, perhaps you might see a thousand clever men, all employed in carving the same design. Of the degradation and deathfulness to the art-intellect of the country involved in such a habit, I have more or less been led to speak before now; but I have not hitherto marked its definite tendency to increase the price of *work*, as such. When men are employed continually in carving the same ornaments, they get into a monotonous and methodical habit of labour--precisely correspondent to that in which they would break stones, or paint house-walls. Of course, what they do so constantly, they do easily; and if you excite them temporarily by an increase of wages, you may get much work done by them in a little time. But, unless so stimulated, men condemned to a monotonous exertion, work--and always, by the laws of human nature, **must** work--only at a tranquil rate, not producing by any means a maximum result in a given time. But if you allow them to vary their designs, and thus interest their heads and hearts in what they are doing, you will find them become eager, first, to get their ideas expressed, and then to finish the expression of them; and the moral energy thus brought to bear on the matter quickens, and therefore cheapens, the production in a most important degree. Sir Thomas Deane, the architect of the new Museum at Oxford, told me, as I passed through Oxford on my way here, that he found that, owing to this cause alone, capitals of various design could be executed cheaper than capitals of similar design (the amount of hand labour in each being the same) by about 30 per cent.

33. Well, that is the first way, then, in which you will employ your intellect well; and the simple observance of this plain rule of political economy will effect a noble revolution in your architecture, such as you cannot at present so much as conceive. Then the second way in which we are to guard against waste is by setting our men to the easiest, and therefore the quickest, work which will answer the purpose. Marble, for instance, lasts quite as long as granite, and is much softer to work; therefore, when you get hold of a good sculptor, give him marble to carve-- not granite.

34. That, you say, is obvious enough. Yes; but it is not so obvious how much of your workmen's time you waste annually in making them cut glass, after it has got hard, when you ought to make them mould it while it is soft. It is not so obvious how much expense you waste in cutting diamonds and rubies, which are the hardest things you can find, into shapes that mean nothing, when the same men might be cutting sandstone and freestone into shapes that meant something. It is not so obvious how much of the artists' time in Italy you waste, by forcing them to make wretched little pictures for you out of crumbs of stone glued together at enormous cost, when the tenth of the time would make good and noble pictures for you out

of water-colour.

35. I could go on giving you almost numberless instances of this great commercial mistake; but I should only weary and confuse you. I therefore commend also this head of our subject to your own meditation, and proceed to the last I named-- the last I shall task your patience with to-night. You know we are now considering how to apply our genius; and we were to do it as economists, in three ways:--

To *various* work;

To *easy* work;

To *lasting* work.

36. This lasting of the work, then, is our final question.

Many of you may perhaps remember that Michael Angelo was once commanded by Pietro di Medici to mould a statue out of snow, and that he obeyed the command.[6] I am glad, and we have all reason to be glad, that such a fancy ever came into the mind of the unworthy prince, and for this cause: that Pietro di Medici then gave, at the period of one great epoch of consummate power in the arts, the perfect, accurate, and intensest possible type of the greatest error which nations and princes can commit, respecting the power of genius entrusted to their guidance. You had there, observe, the strongest genius in the most perfect obedience; capable of iron independence, yet wholly submissive to the patron's will; at once the most highly accomplished and the most original, capable of doing as much as man could do, in any direction that man could ask. And its governor, and guide, and patron sets it to build a statue in snow--to put itself into the service of annihilation--to make a cloud of itself, and pass away from the earth.

[Note 6: See the noble passage on this tradition in "Casa Guidi Windows."]

37. Now this, so precisely and completely done by Pietro di Medici, is what we are all doing, exactly in the degree in which we direct the genius under our patronage to work in more or less perishable materials. So far as we induce painters to work in fading colours, or architects to build with imperfect structure, or in any other way consult only immediate ease and cheapness in the production of what we want, to the exclusion of provident thought as to its permanence and serviceableness in after ages; so far we are forcing our Michael Angelos to carve in snow. The first duty of the economist in art is, to see that no intellect shall thus glitter merely in the manner of hoar-frost; but that it shall be well vitrified, like a painted

window, and shall be set so between shafts of stone and bands of iron, that it shall bear the sunshine upon it, and send the sunshine through it, from generation to generation.

38. I can conceive, however, some political economist to interrupt me here, and say, "If you make your art wear too well, you will soon have too much of it; you will throw your artists quite out of work. Better allow for a little wholesome evanescence--beneficent destruction: let each age provide art for itself, or we shall soon have so many good pictures that we shall not know what to do with them."

Remember, my dear hearers, who are thus thinking, that political economy, like every other subject, cannot be dealt with effectively if we try to solve two questions at a time instead of one. It is one question, how to get plenty of a thing; and another, whether plenty of it will be good for us. Consider these two matters separately; never confuse yourself by interweaving one with the other. It is one question, how to treat your fields so as to get a good harvest; another, whether you wish to have a good harvest, or would rather like to keep up the price of corn. It is one question, how to graft your trees so as to grow most apples; and quite another, whether having such a heap of apples in the storeroom will not make them all rot.

39. Now, therefore, that we are talking only about grafting and growing, pray do not vex yourselves with thinking what you are to do with the pippins. It may be desirable for us to have much art, or little--we will examine that by-and-bye; but just now, let us keep to the simple consideration how to get plenty of good art if we want it. Perhaps it might be just as well that a man of moderate income should be able to possess a good picture, as that any work of real merit should cost 500*l.* or 1,000*l.*; at all events, it is certainly one of the branches of political economy to ascertain how, if we like, we can get things in quantities--plenty of corn, plenty of wine, plenty of gold, or plenty of pictures.

It has just been said, that the first great secret is to produce work that will last. Now, the conditions of work lasting are twofold: it must not only be in materials that will last, but it must be itself of a quality that will last--it must be good enough to bear the test of time. If it is not good, we shall tire of it quickly, and throw it aside--we shall have no pleasure in the accumulation of it. So that the first question of a good art-economist respecting any work is, Will it lose its flavour by keeping? It may be very amusing now, and look much like a work of genius; but what will be its value a hundred years hence?

You cannot always ascertain this. You may get what you fancy to be work of the best quality, and yet find to your astonishment that it won't keep. But of one thing you may be sure, that art which is produced hastily will also perish hastily; and that what is cheapest to you now, is likely to be dearest in the end.

40. I am sorry to say, the great tendency of this age is to expend its genius in perishable art of this kind, as if it were a triumph to burn its thoughts away in bonfires. There is a vast quantity of intellect and of labour consumed annually in our cheap illustrated publications; you triumph in them; and you think it so grand a thing to get so many woodcuts for a penny. Why, woodcuts, penny and all, are as much lost to you as if you had invested your money in gossamer. More lost, for the gossamer could only tickle your face, and glitter in your eyes; it could not catch your feet and trip you up: but the bad art can, and does; for you can't like good woodcuts as long as you look at the bad ones. If we were at this moment to come across a Titian woodcut, or a Duerer woodcut, we should not like it--those of us at least who are accustomed to the cheap work of the day. We don't like, and can't like, **that** long; but when we are tired of one bad cheap thing, we throw it aside and buy another bad cheap thing; and so keep looking at bad things all our lives. Now, the very men who do all that quick bad work for us are capable of doing perfect work. Only, perfect work can't be hurried, and therefore it can't be cheap beyond a certain point. But suppose you pay twelve times as much as you do now, and you have one woodcut for a shilling instead of twelve; and the one woodcut for a shilling is as good as art can be, so that you will never tire of looking at it; and is struck on good paper with good ink, so that you will never wear it out by handling it; while you are sick of your penny-each cuts by the end of the week, and have torn them mostly in half too. Isn't your shilling's worth the best bargain?

41. It is not, however, only in getting prints or woodcuts of the best kind that you will practise economy. There is a certain quality about an original drawing which you cannot get in a woodcut, and the best part of the genius of many men is only expressible in original work, whether with pen or ink--pencil or colours. This is not always the case; but in general, the best men are those who can only express themselves on paper or canvas; and you will therefore, in the long run, get most for your money by buying original work; proceeding on the principle already laid

down, that the best is likely to be the cheapest in the end. Of course, original work cannot be produced under a certain cost. If you want a man to make you a drawing which takes him six days, you must, at all events, keep him for six days in bread and water, fire and lodging; that is the lowest price at which he can do it for you, but that is not very dear: and the best bargain which can possibly be made honestly in art--the very ideal of a cheap purchase to the purchaser--is the original work of a great man fed for as many days as are necessary on bread and water, or perhaps we may say with as many onions as will keep him in good humour. That is the way by which you will always get most for your money; no mechanical multiplication or ingenuity of commercial arrangements will ever get you a better penny's worth of art than that.

42. Without, however, pushing our calculations quite to this prison-discipline extreme, we may lay it down as a rule in art-economy, that original work is, on the whole, cheapest and best worth having. But precisely in proportion to the value of it as a production, becomes the importance of having it executed in permanent materials. And here we come to note the second main error of the day, that we not only ask our workmen for bad art, but we make them put it into bad substance. We have, for example, put a great quantity of genius, within the last twenty years, into water-colour drawing, and we have done this with the most reckless disregard whether either the colours or the paper will stand. In most instances, neither will. By accident, it may happen that the colours in a given drawing have been of good quality, and its paper uninjured by chemical processes. But you take not the least care to ensure these being so; I have myself seen the most destructive changes take place in water-colour drawings within twenty years after they were painted; and from all I can gather respecting the recklessness of modern paper manufacture, my belief is, that though you may still handle an Albert Duerer engraving, two hundred years old, fearlessly, not one-half of that time will have passed over your modern water-colours, before most of them will be reduced to mere white or brown rags; and your descendants, twitching them contemptuously into fragments between finger and thumb, will mutter against you, half in scorn and half in anger, "Those wretched nineteenth century people! they kept vapouring and fuming about the world, doing what they called business, and they couldn't make a sheet of paper that wasn't rotten."

43. And note that this is no unimportant portion of your art economy at this time. Your water-colour painters are becoming every day capable of expressing greater and better things; and their material is especially adapted to the turn of your best artists' minds. The value which you could accumulate in work of this kind would soon become a most important item in the national art-wealth, if only you would take the little pains necessary to secure its permanence. I am inclined to think, myself, that water-colour ought not to be used on paper at all, but only on vellum, and then, if properly taken care of, the drawing would be almost imperishable. Still, paper is a much more convenient material for rapid work; and it is an infinite absurdity not to secure the goodness of its quality, when we could do so without the slightest trouble. Among the many favours which I am going to ask from our paternal government, when we get it, will be that it will supply its little boys with good paper. You have nothing to do but to let the government establish a paper manufactory, under the superintendence of any of our leading chemists, who should be answerable for the safety and completeness of all the processes of the manufacture. The government stamp on the corner of your sheet of drawing-paper, made in the perfect way, should cost you a shilling, which would add something to the revenue; and when you bought a water-colour drawing for fifty or a hundred guineas, you would have merely to look in the corner for your stamp, and pay your extra shilling for the security that your hundred guineas were given really for a drawing, and not for a coloured rag. There need be no monopoly or restriction in the matter; let the paper manufacturers compete with the government, and if people liked to save their shilling, and take their chance, let them; only, the artist and purchaser might then be sure of good material, if they liked, and now they cannot be.

44. I should like also to have a government colour manufactory; though that is not so necessary, as the quality of colour is more within the artist's power of testing, and I have no doubt that any painter may get permanent colour from the respectable manufacturers, if he chooses. I will not attempt to follow the subject out at all as it respects architecture, and our methods of modern building; respecting which I have had occasion to speak before now.

45. But I cannot pass without some brief notice our habit--continually, as it seems to me, gaining strength--of putting a large quantity of thought and work, annually, into things which are either in their nature necessarily perishable, as dress;

or else into compliances with the fashion of the day, in things not necessarily perishable, as plate. I am afraid almost the first idea of a young rich couple setting up
house in London, is, that they must have new plate. Their father's plate may be very
handsome, but the fashion is changed. They will have a new service from the leading manufacturer, and the old plate, except a few apostle spoons, and a cup which
Charles the Second drank a health in to their pretty ancestress, is sent to be melted
down, and made up with new flourishes and fresh lustre. Now, so long as this is
the case--so long, observe, as fashion has influence on the manufacture of plate--so
long *you cannot have a goldsmith's art in this country*. Do you suppose any workman worthy the name will put his brains into a cup, or an urn, which he knows is to
go to the melting-pot in half a score years? He will not; you don't ask or expect it of
him. You ask of him nothing but a little quick handicraft--a clever twist of a handle
here, and a foot there, a convolvulus from the newest school of design, a pheasant
from Landseer's game cards; a couple of sentimental figures for supporters, in the
style of the signs of insurance offices, then a clever touch with the burnisher, and
there's your epergne, the admiration of all the footmen at the wedding-breakfast,
and the torment of some unfortunate youth who cannot see the pretty girl opposite
to him, through its tyrannous branches.

46. But you don't suppose that *that's* goldsmith's work? Goldsmith's work is
made to last, and made with the men's whole heart and soul in it; true goldsmith's
work, when it exists, is generally the means of education of the greatest painters
and sculptors of the day. Francia was a goldsmith; Francia was not his own name,
but that of his master the jeweller; and he signed his pictures almost always, "Francia, the goldsmith," for love of his master; Ghirlandajo was a goldsmith, and was
the master of Michael Angelo; Verrocchio was a goldsmith, and was the master of
Leonardo da Vinci. Ghiberti was a goldsmith, and beat out the bronze gates which
Michael Angelo said might serve for gates of Paradise.[7] But if ever you want work
like theirs again, you must keep it, though it should have the misfortune to become
old-fashioned. You must not break it up, nor melt it any more. There is no economy
in that; you could not easily waste intellect more grievously. Nature may melt her
goldsmith's work at every sunset if she chooses; and beat it out into chased bars
again at every sunrise; but you must not. The way to have a truly noble service of
plate, is to keep adding to it, not melting it. At every marriage, and at every birth,

get a new piece of gold or silver if you will, but with noble workmanship on it, done for all time, and put it among your treasures; that is one of the chief things which gold was made for, and made incorruptible for. When we know a little more of political economy, we shall find that none but partially savage nations need, imperatively, gold for their currency;[8] but gold has been given us, among other things, that we might put beautiful work into its imperishable splendour, and that the artists who have the most wilful fancies may have a material which will drag out, and beat out, as their dreams require, and will hold itself together with fantastic tenacity, whatever rare and delicate service they set it upon.

> [Note 7: Several reasons may account for the fact that goldsmith's work is so wholesome for young artists: first, that it gives great firmness of hand to deal for some time with a solid substance; again, that it induces caution and steadiness--a boy trusted with chalk and paper suffers an immediate temptation to scrawl upon it and play with it, but he dares not scrawl on gold, and he cannot play with it; and, lastly, that it gives great delicacy and precision of touch to work upon minute forms, and to aim at producing richness and finish of design correspondent to the preciousness of the material.]

> [Note 8: See note in Addenda on the nature of property.]

47. So here is one branch of decorative art in which rich people may indulge themselves unselfishly; if they ask for good art in it, they may be sure in buying gold and silver plate that they are enforcing useful education on young artists. But there is another branch of decorative art in which I am sorry to say we cannot, at least under existing circumstances, indulge ourselves, with the hope of doing good to anybody: I mean the great and subtle art of dress.

48. And here I must interrupt the pursuit of our subject for a moment or two, in order to state one of the principles of political economy, which, though it is, I believe, now sufficiently understood and asserted by the leading masters of the science, is not yet, I grieve to say, acted upon by the plurality of those who have the management of riches. Whenever we spend money, we of course set people to work: that is the meaning of spending money; we may, indeed, lose it without employing anybody; but, whenever we spend it, we set a number of people to work, greater or less, of course, according to the rate of wages, but, in the long run, proportioned to the sum we spend. Well, your shallow people, because they see that however they

spend money they are always employing somebody, and, therefore, doing some good, think and say to themselves, that it is all one *how* they spend it--that all their apparently selfish luxury is, in reality, unselfish, and is doing just as much good as if they gave all their money away, or perhaps more good; and I have heard foolish people even declare it as a principle of political economy, that whoever invented a new want[9] conferred a good on the community. I have not words strong enough--at least, I could not, without shocking you, use the words which would be strong enough--to express my estimate of the absurdity and the mischievousness of this popular fallacy. So, putting a great restraint upon myself, and using no hard words, I will simply try to state the nature of it, and the extent of its influence.

[Note 9: See note 5th, in Addenda.]

49. Granted, that whenever we spend money for whatever purpose, we set people to work; and passing by, for the moment, the question whether the work we set them to is all equally healthy and good for them, we will assume that whenever we spend a guinea we provide an equal number of people with healthy maintenance for a given time. But, by the way in which we spend it, we entirely direct the labour of those people during that given time. We become their masters or mistresses, and we compel them to produce, within a certain period, a certain article. Now, that article may be a useful and lasting one, or it may be a useless and perishable one--it may be one useful to the whole community, or useful only to ourselves. And our selfishness and folly, or our virtue and prudence, are shown, not by our spending money, but by our spending it for the wrong or the right thing; and we are wise and kind, not in maintaining a certain number of people for a given period, but only in requiring them to produce during that period, the kind of things which shall be useful to society, instead of those which are only useful to ourselves.

50. Thus, for instance: if you are a young lady, and employ a certain number of sempstresses for a given time, in making a given number of simple and serviceable dresses--suppose, seven; of which you can wear one yourself for half the winter, and give six away to poor girls who have none, you are spending your money unselfishly. But if you employ the same number of sempstresses for the same number of days, in making four, or five, or six beautiful flounces for your own ball-dress--flounces which will clothe no one but yourself, and which you will yourself be unable to wear at more than one ball--you are employing your money selfishly. You

have maintained, indeed, in each case, the same number of people; but in the one case you have directed their labour to the service of the community; in the other case you have consumed it wholly upon yourself. I don't say you are never to do so; I don't say you ought not sometimes to think of yourselves only, and to make yourselves as pretty as you can; only do not confuse coquettishness with benevolence, nor cheat yourselves into thinking that all the finery you can wear is so much put into the hungry mouths of those beneath you: it is not so; it is what you yourselves, whether you will or no, must sometimes instinctively feel it to be--it is what those who stand shivering in the streets, forming a line to watch you as you step out of your carriages, *know* it to be; those fine dresses do not mean that so much has been put into their mouths, but that so much has been taken out of their mouths.

51. The real politico-economical signification of every one of those beautiful toilettes, is just this: that you have had a certain number of people put for a certain number of days wholly under your authority, by the sternest of slave-masters--hunger and cold; and you have said to them, "I will feed you, indeed, and clothe you, and give you fuel for so many days; but during those days you shall work for me only: your little brothers need clothes, but you shall make none for them: your sick friend needs clothes, but you shall make none for her: you yourself will soon need another and a warmer dress, but you shall make none for yourself. You shall make nothing but lace and roses for me; for this fortnight to come, you shall work at the patterns and petals, and then I will crush and consume them away in an hour." You will perhaps answer--"It may not be particularly benevolent to do this, and we won't call it so; but at any rate we do no wrong in taking their labour when we pay them their wages: if we pay for their work, we have a right to it."

52. No;--a thousand times no. The labour which you have paid for, does indeed become, by the act of purchase, your own labour: you have bought the hands and the time of those workers; they are, by right and justice, your own hands, your own time. But have you a right to spend your own time, to work with your own hands, only for your own advantage?--much more, when, by purchase, you have invested your own person with the strength of others; and added to your own life, a part of the life of others? You may, indeed, to a certain extent, use their labour for your delight: remember, I am making no general assertions against splendour of dress, or pomp of accessories of life; on the contrary, there are many reasons for thinking

that we do not at present attach enough importance to beautiful dress, as one of the means of influencing general taste and character. But I *do* say, that you must weigh the value of what you ask these workers to produce for you in its own distinct balance; that on its own worthiness or desirableness rests the question of your kindness, and not merely on the fact of your having employed people in producing it: and I say further, that as long as there are cold and nakedness in the land around you, so long there can be no question at all but that splendour of dress is a crime. In due time, when we have nothing better to set people to work at, it may be right to let them make lace and cut jewels; but as long as there are any who have no blankets for their beds, and no rags for their bodies, so long it is blanket-making and tailoring we must set people to work at--not lace.

53. And it would be strange, if at any great assembly which, while it dazzled the young and the thoughtless, beguiled the gentler hearts that beat beneath the embroidery, with a placid sensation of luxurious benevolence--as if by all that they wore in waywardness of beauty, comfort had been first given to the distressed, and aid to the indigent; it would be strange, I say, if, for a moment, the spirits of Truth and of Terror, which walk invisibly among the masques of the earth, would lift the dimness from our erring thoughts, and show us how--inasmuch as the sums exhausted for that magnificence would have given back the failing breath to many an unsheltered outcast on moor and street--they who wear it have literally entered into partnership with Death; and dressed themselves in his spoils. Yes, if the veil could be lifted not only from your thoughts, but from your human sight, you would see--the angels do see--on those gay white dresses of yours, strange dark spots, and crimson patterns that you knew not of--spots of the inextinguishable red that all the seas cannot wash away; yes, and among the pleasant flowers that crown your fair heads, and glow on your wreathed hair, you would see that one weed was always twisted which no one thought of--the grass that grows on graves.

54. It was not, however, this last, this clearest and most appalling view of our subject, that I intended to ask you to take this evening; only it is impossible to set any part of the matter in its true light, until we go to the root of it. But the point which it is our special business to consider is, not whether costliness of dress is contrary to charity; but whether it is not contrary to mere worldly wisdom: whether, even supposing we knew that splendour of dress did not cost suffering or hunger,

we might not put the splendour better in other things than dress. And, supposing our mode of dress were really graceful or beautiful, this might be a very doubtful question; for I believe true nobleness of dress to be an important means of education, as it certainly is a necessity to any nation which wishes to possess living art, concerned with portraiture of human nature. No good historical painting ever yet existed, or ever can exist, where the dresses of the people of the time are not beautiful: and had it not been for the lovely and fantastic dressing of the thirteenth to the sixteenth centuries, neither French, nor Florentine, nor Venetian art could have risen to anything like the rank it reached. Still, even then, the best dressing was never the costliest; and its effect depended much more on its beautiful and, in early times, modest, arrangement, and on the simple and lovely masses of its colour, than on gorgeousness of clasp or embroidery.

55. Whether we can ever return to any of those more perfect types of form, is questionable; but there can be no more question that all the money we spend on the forms of dress at present worn, is, so far as any good purpose is concerned, wholly lost. Mind, in saying this, I reckon among good purposes the purpose which young ladies are said sometimes to entertain--of being married; but they would be married quite as soon (and probably to wiser and better husbands) by dressing quietly, as by dressing brilliantly: and I believe it would only be needed to lay fairly and largely before them the real good which might be effected by the sums they spend in toilettes, to make them trust at once only to their bright eyes and braided hair for all the mischief they have a mind to. I wish we could, for once, get the statistics of a London season. There was much complaining talk in Parliament, last week, of the vast sum the nation has given for the best Paul Veronese in Venice--14,000*l.*: I wonder what the nation meanwhile has given for its ball-dresses! Suppose we could see the London milliners' bills, simply for unnecessary breadths of slip and flounce, from April to July; I wonder whether 14,000*l.* would cover *them*. But the breadths of slip and flounce are by this time as much lost and vanished as last year's snow; only they have done less good: but the Paul Veronese will last for centuries, if we take care of it; and yet, we grumble at the price given for the painting, while no one grumbles at the price of pride.

56. Time does not permit me to go into any farther illustration of the various modes in which we build our statue out of snow, and waste our labour on things

that vanish. I must leave you to follow out the subject for yourselves, as I said I should, and proceed, in our next lecture, to examine the two other branches of our subject--namely, how to accumulate our art, and how to distribute it. But, in closing, as we have been much on the topic of good government, both of ourselves and others, let me just give you one more illustration of what it means, from that old art of which, next evening, I shall try to convince you that the value, both moral and mercantile, is greater than we usually suppose.

57. One of the frescoes by Ambrozio Lorenzetti, in the town-hall of Siena, represents, by means of symbolical figures, the principles of Good Civic Government and of Good Government in general. The figure representing this noble Civic Government is enthroned, and surrounded by figures representing the Virtues, variously supporting or administering its authority. Now, observe what work is given to each of these virtues. Three winged ones--Faith, Hope, and Charity--surround the head of the figure; not in mere compliance with the common and heraldic laws of precedence among Virtues, such as we moderns observe habitually, but with peculiar purpose on the part of the painter. Faith, as thus represented ruling the thoughts of the Good Governor, does not mean merely religious faith, understood in those times to be necessary to all persons--governed no less than governors--but it means the faith which enables work to be carried out steadily, in spite of adverse appearances and expediencies; the faith in great principles, by which a civic ruler looks past all the immediate checks and shadows that would daunt a common man, knowing that what is rightly done will have a right issue, and holding his way in spite of pullings at his cloak and whisperings in his ear, enduring, as having in him a faith which is evidence of things unseen.

58. And Hope, in like manner, is here not the heavenward hope which ought to animate the hearts of all men; but she attends upon Good Government, to show that all such government is *expectant* as well as *conservative*; that if it ceases to be hopeful of better things, it ceases to be a wise guardian of present things: that it ought never, as long as the world lasts, to be wholly content with any existing state of institution or possession, but to be hopeful still of more wisdom and power; not clutching at it restlessly or hastily, but feeling that its real life consists in steady ascent from high to higher: conservative, indeed, and jealously conservative of old things, but conservative of them as pillars, not as pinnacles--as aids, but not as idols;

and hopeful chiefly, and active, in times of national trial or distress, according to those first and notable words describing the queenly nation: "She riseth, ***while it is yet night***."

59. And again, the winged Charity which is attendant on Good Government has, in this fresco, a peculiar office. Can you guess what? If you consider the character of contest which so often takes place among kings for their crowns, and the selfish and tyrannous means they commonly take to aggrandize or secure their power, you will, perhaps, be surprised to hear that the office of Charity is to crown the King. And yet, if you think of it a little, you will see the beauty of the thought which sets her in this function: since, in the first place, all the authority of a good governor should be desired by him only for the good of his people, so that it is only Love that makes him accept or guard his crown: in the second place, his chief greatness consists in the exercise of this love, and he is truly to be revered only so far as his acts and thoughts are those of kindness; so that Love is the light of his crown, as well as the giver of it: lastly, because his strength depends on the affections of his people, and it is only their love which can securely crown him, and for ever. So that Love is the strength of his crown as well as the light of it.

60. Then, surrounding the King, or in various obedience to him, appear the dependent virtues, as Fortitude, Temperance, Truth, and other attendant spirits, of all which I cannot now give account, wishing you only to notice the one to whom are entrusted the guidance and administration of the public revenues. Can you guess which it is likely to be? Charity, you would have thought, should have something to do with the business; but not so, for she is too hot to attend carefully to it. Prudence, perhaps, you think of in the next place. No, she is too timid, and loses opportunities in making up her mind. Can it be Liberality then? No: Liberality is entrusted with some small sums; but she is a bad accountant, and is allowed no important place in the exchequer. But the treasures are given in charge to a virtue of which we hear too little in modern times, as distinct from others; Magnanimity: largeness of heart: not softness or weakness of heart, mind you--but capacity of heart--the great ***measuring*** virtue, which weighs in heavenly balances all that may be given, and all that may be gained; and sees how to do noblest things in noblest ways: which of two goods comprehends and therefore chooses the greater: which of two personal sacrifices dares and accepts the larger: which, out of the avenues of beneficence, treads

always that which opens farthest into the blue fields of futurity: that character, in fine, which, in those words taken by us at first for the description of a Queen among the nations, looks less to the present power than to the distant promise; "Strength and honour are in her clothing,--and she shall rejoice IN TIME TO COME."

LECTURE II.
THE ACCUMULATION AND DISTRIBUTION OF ART.

Continuation of the previous Lecture; delivered July 13, 1857.

61. The heads of our subject which remain for our consideration this evening are, you will remember, the accumulation and the distribution of works of art. Our complete inquiry fell into four divisions--first, how to get our genius; then, how to apply our genius; then, how to accumulate its results; and lastly, how to distribute them. We considered, last evening, how to discover and apply it;--we have to-night to examine the modes of its preservation and distribution.

62. III. ACCUMULATION.--And now, in the outset, it will be well to face that objection which we put aside a little while ago; namely, that perhaps it is not well to have a great deal of good art; and that it should not be made too cheap.

"Nay," I can imagine some of the more generous among you exclaiming, "we will not trouble you to disprove that objection; of course it is a selfish and base one: good art, as well as other good things, ought to be made as cheap as possible, and put as far as we can within the reach of everybody."

63. Pardon me, I am not prepared to admit that. I rather side with the selfish objectors, and believe that art ought not to be made cheap, beyond a certain point; for the amount of pleasure that you can receive from any great work, depends wholly on the quantity of attention and energy of mind you can bring to bear upon it. Now, that attention and energy depend much more on the freshness of the thing than you would at all suppose; unless you very carefully studied the movements of your own minds. If you see things of the same kind and of equal value very frequently, your reverence for them is infallibly diminished, your powers of attention get gradually

wearied, and your interest and enthusiasm worn out; and you cannot in that state bring to any given work the energy necessary to enjoy it. If, indeed, the question were only between enjoying a great many pictures each a little, or one picture very much, the sum of enjoyment being in each case the same, you might rationally desire to possess rather the larger quantity than the small; both because one work of art always in some sort illustrates another, and because quantity diminishes the chances of destruction.

64. But the question is not a merely arithmetical one of this kind. Your fragments of broken admirations will not, when they are put together, make up one whole admiration; two and two, in this case, do not make four, nor anything like four. Your good picture, or book, or work of art of any kind, is always in some degree fenced and closed about with difficulty. You may think of it as of a kind of cocoanut, with very often rather an unseemly shell, but good milk and kernel inside. Now, if you possess twenty cocoanuts, and being thirsty, go impatiently from one to the other, giving only a single scratch with the point of your knife to the shell of each, you will get no milk from all the twenty. But if you leave nineteen of them alone, and give twenty cuts to the shell of one, you will get through it, and at the milk of it. And the tendency of the human mind is always to get tired before it has made its twenty cuts; and to try another nut: and moreover, even if it has perseverance enough to crack its nuts, it is sure to try to eat too many, and to choke itself. Hence, it is wisely appointed for us that few of the things we desire can be had without considerable labour, and at considerable intervals of time. We cannot generally get our dinner without working for it, and that gives us appetite for it, we cannot get our holiday without waiting for it, and that gives us zest for it; and we ought not to get our picture without paying for it, and that gives us a mind to look at it.

65. Nay, I will even go so far as to say that we ought not to get books too cheaply. No book, I believe, is ever worth half so much to its reader as one that has been coveted for a year at a bookstall, and bought out of saved halfpence; and perhaps a day or two's fasting. That's the way to get at the cream of a book. And I should say more on this matter, and protest as energetically as I could against the plague of cheap literature, with which we are just now afflicted, but that I fear your calling me to order, as being unpractical, because I don't quite see my way at pres-

ent to making everybody fast for their books. But one may see that a thing is desirable and possible, even though one may not at once know the best way to it,--and in my island of Barataria, when I get it well into order, I assure you no book shall be sold for less than a pound sterling; if it can be published cheaper than that, the surplus shall all go into my treasury, and save my subjects taxation in other directions; only people really poor, who cannot pay the pound, shall be supplied with the books they want for nothing, in a certain limited quantity. I haven't made up my mind about the number yet, and there are several other points in the system yet unsettled; when they are all determined, if you will allow me, I will come and give you another lecture, on the political economy of literature.[10]

[Note 10: See note 6th, in Addenda.]

66. Meantime, returning to our immediate subject, I say to my generous hearers, who want to shower Titians and Turners upon us, like falling leaves, "Pictures ought not to be too cheap;" but in much stronger tone I would say to those who want to keep up the prices of pictorial property, that pictures ought not to be too dear--that is to say, not as dear as they are. For, as matters at present stand, it is wholly impossible for any man in the ordinary circumstances of English life to possess himself of a piece of great art. A modern drawing of average merit, or a first-class engraving, may, perhaps, not without some self-reproach, be purchased out of his savings by a man of narrow income; but a satisfactory example of first-rate art--masterhands' work--is wholly out of his reach. And we are so accustomed to look upon this as the natural course and necessity of things, that we never set ourselves in any wise to diminish the evil; and yet it is an evil perfectly capable of diminution.

67. It is an evil precisely similar in kind to that which existed in the Middle Ages, respecting good books, and which everybody then, I suppose, thought as natural as we do now our small supply of good pictures. You could not then study the work of a great historian, or great poet, any more than you can now study that of a great painter, but at heavy cost. If you wanted a book, you had to get it written out for you, or to write it out for yourself. But printing came, and the poor man may read his Dante and his Homer; and Dante and Homer are none the worse for that. But it is only in literature that private persons of moderate fortune can possess and study greatness: they can study at home no greatness in art; and the object of that

accumulation which we are at present aiming at, as our third object in political economy, is to bring great art in some degree within the reach of the multitude; and, both in larger and more numerous galleries than we now possess, and by distribution, according to his wealth and wish, in each man's home, to render the influence of art somewhat correspondent in extent to that of literature. Here, then, is the subtle balance which your economist has to strike: to accumulate so much art as to be able to give the whole nation a supply of it, according to its need, and yet to regulate its distribution so that there shall be no glut of it, nor contempt.

68. A difficult balance, indeed, for us to hold, if it were left merely to our skill to poise; but the just point between poverty and profusion has been fixed for us accurately by the wise laws of Providence. If you carefully watch for all the genius you can detect, apply it to good service, and then reverently preserve what it produces, you will never have too little art; and if, on the other hand, you never force an artist to work hurriedly, for daily bread, nor imperfectly, because you would rather have showy works than complete ones, you will never have too much. Do not force the multiplication of art, and you will not have it too cheap; do not wantonly destroy it, and you will not have it too dear.

69. "But who wantonly destroys it?" you will ask. Why, we all do. Perhaps you thought, when I came to this part of our subject, corresponding to that set forth in our housewife's economy by the "keeping her embroidery from the moth," that I was going to tell you only how to take better care of pictures, how to clean them, and varnish them, and where to put them away safely when you went out of town. Ah, not at all. The utmost I have to ask of you is, that you will not pull them to pieces, and trample them under your feet. "What!" you will say, "when do we do such things? Haven't we built a perfectly beautiful gallery for all the pictures we have to take care of?" Yes, you have, for the pictures which are definitely sent to Manchester to be taken care of. But there are quantities of pictures out of Manchester which it is your business, and mine too, to take care of no less than of these, and which we are at this moment employing ourselves in pulling to pieces by deputy. I will tell you what they are, and where they are, in a minute; only first let me state one more of those main principles of political economy on which the matter hinges.

70. I must begin a little apparently wide of the mark, and ask you to reflect if there is any way in which we waste money more in England than in building fine

tombs? Our respect for the dead, when they are *just* dead, is something wonderful, and the way we show it more wonderful still. We show it with black feathers and black horses; we show it with black dresses and bright heraldries; we show it with costly obelisks and sculptures of sorrow, which spoil half of our most beautiful cathedrals. We show it with frightful gratings and vaults, and lids of dismal stone, in the midst of the quiet grass; and last, and not least, we show it by permitting ourselves to tell any number of lies we think amiable or credible, in the epitaph. This feeling is common to the poor as well as the rich; and we all know how many a poor family will nearly ruin themselves, to testify their respect for some member of it in his coffin, whom they never much cared for when he was out of it; and how often it happens that a poor old woman will starve herself to death, in order that she may be respectably buried.

71. Now, this being one of the most complete and special ways of wasting money,--no money being less productive of good, or of any percentage whatever, than that which we shake away from the ends of undertakers' plumes,--it is of course the duty of all good economists, and kind persons, to prove and proclaim continually, to the poor as well as the rich, that respect for the dead is not really shown by laying great stones on them to tell us where they are laid; but by remembering where they are laid, without a stone to help us; trusting them to the sacred grass and saddened flowers; and still more, that respect and love are shown to them, not by great monuments to them which we build with *our* hands, but by letting the monuments stand, which they built with *their own*. And this is the point now in question.

72. Observe, there are two great reciprocal duties concerning industry, constantly to be exchanged between the living and the dead. We, as we live and work, are to be always thinking of those who are to come after us; that what we do may be serviceable, as far as we can make it so, to them, as well as to us. Then, when we die, it is the duty of those who come after us to accept this work of ours with thanks and remembrance, not thrusting it aside or tearing it down the moment they think they have no use for it. And each generation will only be happy or powerful to the pitch that it ought to be, in fulfilling these two duties to the Past and the Future. Its own work will never be rightly done, even for itself--never good, or noble, or pleasurable to its own eyes--if it does not prepare it also for the eyes of generations yet

to come. And its own possessions will never be enough for it, and its own wisdom never enough for it, unless it avails itself gratefully and tenderly of the treasures and the wisdom bequeathed to it by its ancestors.

73. For, be assured, that all the best things and treasures of this world are not to be produced by each generation for itself; but we are all intended, not to carve our work in snow that will melt, but each and all of us to be continually rolling a great white gathering snowball, higher and higher--larger and larger--along the Alps of human power. Thus the science of nations is to be accumulative from father to son: each learning a little more and a little more; each receiving all that was known, and adding its own gain: the history and poetry of nations are to be accumulative; each generation treasuring the history and the songs of its ancestors, adding its own history and its own songs: and the art of nations is to be accumulative, just as science and history are; the work of living men is not superseding, but building itself upon the work of the past. Nearly every great and intellectual race of the world has produced, at every period of its career, an art with some peculiar and precious character about it, wholly unattainable by any other race, and at any other time; and the intention of Providence concerning that art, is evidently that it should all grow together into one mighty temple; the rough stones and the smooth all finding their place, and rising, day by day, in richer and higher pinnacles to heaven.

74. Now, just fancy what a position the world, considered as one great workroom--one great factory in the form of a globe--would have been in by this time, if it had in the least understood this duty, or been capable of it. Fancy what we should have had around us now, if, instead of quarrelling and fighting over their work, the nations had aided each other in their work, or if even in their conquests, instead of effacing the memorials of those they succeeded and subdued, they had guarded the spoils of their victories. Fancy what Europe would be now, if the delicate statues and temples of the Greeks--if the broad roads and massy walls of the Romans--if the noble and pathetic architecture of the middle ages, had not been ground to dust by mere human rage. You talk of the scythe of Time, and the tooth of Time: I tell you, Time is scytheless and toothless; it is we who gnaw like the worm--we who smite like the scythe. It is ourselves who abolish--ourselves who consume: we are the mildew, and the flame; and the soul of man is to its own work as the moth that frets when it cannot fly, and as the hidden flame that blasts where it cannot illuminate.

All these lost treasures of human intellect have been wholly destroyed by human industry of destruction; the marble would have stood its two thousand years as well in the polished statue as in the Parian cliff; but we men have ground it to powder, and mixed it with our own ashes. The walls and the ways would have stood--it is we who have left not one stone upon another, and restored its pathlessness to the desert; the great cathedrals of old religion would have stood--it is we who have dashed down the carved work with axes and hammers, and bid the mountain-grass bloom upon the pavement, and the sea-winds chant in the galleries.

75. You will perhaps think all this was somehow necessary for the development of the human race. I cannot stay now to dispute that, though I would willingly; but do you think it is *still* necessary for that development? Do you think that in this nineteenth century it is still necessary for the European nations to turn all the places where their principal art-treasures are into battle-fields? For that is what they are doing even while I speak; the great firm of the world is managing its business at this moment, just as it has done in past time. Imagine what would be the thriving circumstances of a manufacturer of some delicate produce--suppose glass, or china--in whose workshop and exhibition rooms all the workmen and clerks began fighting at least once a day, first blowing off the steam, and breaking all the machinery they could reach; and then making fortresses of all the cupboards, and attacking and defending the show-tables, the victorious party finally throwing everything they could get hold of out of the window, by way of showing their triumph, and the poor manufacturer picking up and putting away at last a cup here and a handle there. A fine prosperous business that would be, would it not? and yet that is precisely the way the great manufacturing firm of the world carries on its business.

76. It has so arranged its political squabbles for the last six or seven hundred years, that not one of them could be fought out but in the midst of its most precious art; and it so arranges them to this day. For example, if I were asked to lay my finger, in a map of the world, on the spot of the world's surface which contained at this moment the most singular concentration of art-teaching and art-treasure, I should lay it on the name of the town of Verona. Other cities, indeed, contain more works of carriageable art, but none contain so much of the glorious local art, and of the springs and sources of art, which can by no means be made subjects of package or porterage, nor, I grieve to say, of salvage. Verona possesses, in the first place, not the

largest, but the most perfect and intelligible Roman amphitheatre that exists, still unbroken in circle of step, and strong in succession of vault and arch: it contains minor Roman monuments, gateways, theatres, baths, wrecks of temples, which give the streets of its suburbs a character of antiquity unexampled elsewhere, except in Rome itself. But it contains, in the next place, what Rome does not contain--perfect examples of the great twelfth-century Lombardic architecture, which was the root of all the mediaeval art of Italy, without which no Giottos, no Angelicos, no Raphaels would have been possible: it contains that architecture, not in rude forms, but in the most perfect and loveliest types it ever attained--contains those, not in ruins, nor in altered and hardly decipherable fragments, but in churches perfect from porch to apse, with all their carving fresh, their pillars firm, their joints unloosened. Besides these, it includes examples of the great thirteenth and fourteenth-century Gothic of Italy, not merely perfect, but elsewhere unrivalled. At Rome, the Roman--at Pisa, the Lombard--architecture may be seen in greater or in equal nobleness; but not at Rome, nor Pisa, nor Florence, nor in any city of the world, is there a great mediaeval Gothic like the Gothic of Verona. Elsewhere, it is either less pure in type or less lovely in completion: only at Verona may you see it in the simplicity of its youthful power, and the tenderness of its accomplished beauty. And Verona possesses, in the last place, the loveliest Renaissance architecture of Italy, not disturbed by pride, nor defiled by luxury, but rising in fair fulfilment of domestic service, serenity of effortless grace, and modesty of home seclusion; its richest work given to the windows that open on the narrowest streets and most silent gardens. All this she possesses, in the midst of natural scenery such as assuredly exists nowhere else in the habitable globe--a wild Alpine river foaming at her feet, from whose shore the rocks rise in a great crescent, dark with cypress, and misty with olive: illimitably, from before her southern gates, the tufted plains of Italy sweep and fade in golden light; around her, north and west, the Alps crowd in crested troops, and the winds of Benacus bear to her the coolness of their snows.

77. And this is the city--such, and possessing such things as these--at whose gates the decisive battles of Italy are fought continually: three days her towers trembled with the echo of the cannon of Arcola; heaped pebbles of the Mincio divide her fields to this hour with lines of broken rampart, whence the tide of war rolled back to Novara; and now on that crescent of her eastern cliffs, whence the

full moon used to rise through the bars of the cypresses in her burning summer twi-lights, touching with soft increase of silver light the rosy marbles of her balconies,--along the ridge of that encompassing rock, other circles are increasing now, white and pale; walled towers of cruel strength, sable-spotted with cannon-courses. I tell you, I have seen, when the thunderclouds came down on those Italian hills, and all their crags were dipped in the dark, terrible purple, as if the winepress of the wrath of God had stained their mountain-raiment--I have seen the hail fall in Italy till the forest branches stood stripped and bare as if blasted by the locust; but the white hail never fell from those clouds of heaven as the black hail will fall from the clouds of hell, if ever one breath of Italian life stirs again in the streets of Verona.

78. Sad as you will feel this to be, I do not say that you can directly prevent it; you cannot drive the Austrians out of Italy, nor prevent them from building forts where they choose. But I do say,[11] that you, and I, and all of us, ought to be both acting and feeling with a full knowledge and understanding of these things; and that, without trying to excite revolutions or weaken governments, we may give our own thoughts and help, so as in a measure to prevent needless destruction. We should do this, if we only realized the thing thoroughly. You drive out day by day through your own pretty suburbs, and you think only of making, with what money you have to spare, your gateways handsomer, and your carriage-drives wider--and your drawing-rooms more splendid, having a vague notion that you are all the while patronizing and advancing art; and you make no effort to conceive the fact that, within a few hours' journey of you, there are gateways and drawing-rooms which might just as well be yours as these, all built already; gateways built by the greatest masters of sculpture that ever struck marble; drawing-rooms, painted by Titian and Veronese; and you won't accept nor save these as they are, but you will rather fetch the house-painter from over the way, and let Titian and Veronese house the rats.

[Note 11: The reader can hardly but remember Mrs. Browning's beautiful appeal for Italy, made on the occasion of the first great Exhibition of Art in England:--

Magi of the east and of the west,
Your incense, gold, and myrrh are excellent!--
What gifts for Christ, then, bring ye with the rest?
Your hands have worked well. Is your courage spent
In handwork only? Have you nothing best,

Which generous souls may perfect and present,
And He shall thank the givers for? no light
Of teaching, liberal nations, for the poor,
Who sit in darkness when it is not night?
No cure for wicked children? Christ,--no cure,
No help for women, sobbing out of sight
Because men made the laws? no brothel-lure
Burnt out by popular lightnings? Hast thou found
No remedy, my England, for such woes?
No outlet, Austria, for the scourged and bound,
No call back for the exiled? no repose,
Russia for knouted Poles worked underground,
And gentle ladies bleached among the snows?
No mercy for the slave, America?
No hope for Rome, free France, chivalric France?
Alas, great nations have great shames, I say.
No pity, O world, no tender utterance
Of benediction, and prayers stretched this way
For poor Italia, baffled by mischance?
O gracious nations, give some ear to me!
You all go to your Fair, and I am one
Who at the roadside of humanity
Beseech your alms,--God's justice to be done.

So, prosper!]

79. "Yes," of course, you answer; "we want nice houses here, not houses in Verona. What should we do with houses in Verona?" And I answer, do precisely what you do with the most expensive part of your possessions here: take pride in them--only a noble pride. You know well, when you examine your own hearts, that the greater part of the sums you spend on possessions is spent for pride. Why are your carriages nicely painted and finished outside? You don't see the outsides as you sit in them--the outsides are for other people to see. Why are your exteriors of houses so well finished, your furniture so polished and costly, but for other people to see? You are just as comfortable yourselves, writing on your old friend of a desk, with the white cloudings in his leather, and using the light of a window which is nothing but a hole in the brick wall. And all that is desirable to be done in this matter is merely to take pride in preserving great art, instead of in producing mean art; pride in the possession of precious and enduring things, a little way off, instead of slight and perishing things near at hand. You know, in old English times, our kings liked

to have lordships and dukedoms abroad: and why should not your merchant princes like to have lordships and estates abroad? Believe me, rightly understood, it would be a prouder, and in the full sense of our English word, more "respectable" thing to be lord of a palace at Verona, or of a cloister full of frescoes at Florence, than to have a file of servants dressed in the finest liveries that ever tailor stitched, as long as would reach from here to Bolton:--yes, and a prouder thing to send people to travel in Italy, who would have to say every now and then, of some fair piece of art, "Ah! this was **kept** here for us by the good people of Manchester," than to bring them travelling all the way here, exclaiming of your various art treasures, "These were **brought** here for us, (not altogether without harm) by the good people of Manchester."

80. "Ah!" but you say, "the Art Treasures Exhibition will pay; but Veronese palaces won't." Pardon me. They **would** pay, less directly, but far more richly. Do you suppose it is in the long run good for Manchester, or good for England, that the Continent should be in the state it is? Do you think the perpetual fear of revolution, or the perpetual repression of thought and energy that clouds and encumbers the nations of Europe, is eventually profitable for **us**? Were we any the better of the course of affairs in '48? or has the stabling of the dragoon horses in the great houses of Italy any distinct effect in the promotion of the cotton-trade? Not so. But every stake that you could hold in the stability of the Continent, and every effort that you could make to give example of English habits and principles on the Continent, and every kind deed that you could do in relieving distress and preventing despair on the Continent, would have tenfold reaction on the prosperity of England, and open and urge, in a thousand unforeseen directions, the sluices of commerce and the springs of industry.

81. I could press, if I chose, both these motives upon you, of pride and self-interest, with more force, but these are not motives which ought to be urged upon you at all. The only motive that I ought to put before you is simply that it would be right to do this; that the holding of property abroad, and the personal efforts of Englishmen to redeem the condition of foreign nations, are among the most direct pieces of duty which our wealth renders incumbent upon us. I do not--and in all truth and deliberateness I say this--I do not know anything more ludicrous among the self-deceptions of well-meaning people than their notion of patriotism, as re-

quiring them to limit their efforts to the good of their own country;--the notion that charity is a geographical virtue, and that what it is holy and righteous to do for people on one bank of a river, it is quite improper and unnatural to do for people on the other. It will be a wonderful thing, some day or other, for the Christian world to remember, that it went on thinking for two thousand years that neighbours were neighbours at Jerusalem, but not at Jericho; a wonderful thing for us English to reflect, in after-years, how long it was before we could shake hands with anybody across that shallow salt wash, which the very chalk-dust of its two shores whitens from Folkestone to Ambleteuse.

82. Nor ought the motive of gratitude, as well as that of mercy, to be without its influence on you, who have been the first to ask to see, and the first to show to us, the treasures which this poor lost Italy has given to England. Remember, all these things that delight you here were hers--hers either in fact or in teaching; hers, in fact, are all the most powerful and most touching paintings of old time that now glow upon your walls; hers in teaching are all the best and greatest of descendant souls--your Reynolds and your Gainsborough never could have painted but for Venice; and the energies which have given the only true life to your existing art were first stirred by voices of the dead that haunted the Sacred Field of Pisa.

Well, all these motives for some definite course of action on our part towards foreign countries rest upon very serious facts; too serious, perhaps you will think, to be interfered with; for we are all of us in the habit of leaving great things alone, as if Providence would mind them, and attending ourselves only to little things which we know, practically, Providence doesn't mind unless we do. We are ready enough to give care to the growing of pines and lettuces, knowing that they don't grow Providentially sweet or large unless we look after them; but we don't give any care to the good of Italy or Germany, because we think that they will grow Providentially happy without any of our meddling.

83. Let us leave the great things, then, and think of little things; not of the destruction of whole provinces in war, which it may not be any business of ours to prevent; but of the destruction of poor little pictures in peace, from which it surely would not be much out of our way to save them. You know I said, just now, we were all of us engaged in pulling pictures to pieces by deputy, and you did not believe me. Consider, then, this similitude of ourselves. Suppose you saw (as I doubt

not you often do see) a prudent and kind young lady sitting at work, in the corner of a quiet room, knitting comforters for her cousins, and that just outside, in the hall, you saw a cat and her kittens at play among the family pictures; amusing themselves especially with the best Vandykes, by getting on the tops of the frames, and then scrambling down the canvases by their claws; and on some one's informing the young lady of these proceedings of the cat and kittens, suppose she answered that it wasn't her cat, but her sister's, and the pictures weren't hers, but her uncle's, and she couldn't leave her work, for she had to make so many pairs of comforters before dinner. Would you not say that the prudent and kind young lady was, on the whole, answerable for the additional touches of claw on the Vandykes?

84. Now, that is precisely what we prudent and kind English are doing, only on a larger scale. Here we sit in Manchester, hard at work, very properly, making comforters for our cousins all over the world. Just outside there in the hall--that beautiful marble hall of Italy--the cats and kittens and monkeys are at play among the pictures: I assure you, in the course of the fifteen years in which I have been working in those places in which the most precious remnants of European art exist, a sensation, whether I would or no, was gradually made distinct and deep in my mind, that I was living and working in the midst of a den of monkeys;--sometimes amiable and affectionate monkeys, with all manner of winning ways and kind intentions,--more frequently selfish and malicious monkeys; but, whatever their disposition, squabbling continually about nuts, and the best places on the barren sticks of trees; and that all this monkeys' den was filled, by mischance, with precious pictures, and the witty and wilful beasts were always wrapping themselves up and going to sleep in pictures, or tearing holes in them to grin through; or tasting them and spitting them out again, or twisting them up into ropes and making swings of them; and that sometimes only, by watching one's opportunity, and bearing a scratch or a bite, one could rescue the corner of a Tintoret, or Paul Veronese, and push it through the bars into a place of safety.

85. Literally, I assure you, this was, and this is, the fixed impression on my mind of the state of matters in Italy. And see how. The professors of art in Italy, having long followed a method of study peculiar to themselves, have at last arrived at a form of art peculiar to themselves; very different from that which was arrived at by Correggio and Titian. Naturally, the professors like their own form the best;

and, as the old pictures are generally not so startling to the eye as the modern ones, the dukes and counts who possess them, and who like to see their galleries look new and fine (and are persuaded also that a celebrated chef-d'oeuvre ought always to catch the eye at a quarter of a mile off), believe the professors who tell them their sober pictures are quite faded, and good for nothing, and should all be brought bright again; and, accordingly, give the sober pictures to the professors, to be put right by rules of art. Then, the professors repaint the old pictures in all the principal places, leaving perhaps only a bit of background to set off their own work. And thus the professors come to be generally figured, in my mind, as the monkeys who tear holes in the pictures, to grin through. Then the picture-dealers, who live by the pictures, cannot sell them to the English in their old and pure state; all the good work must be covered with new paint, and varnished so as to look like one of the professorial pictures in the great gallery, before it is saleable. And thus the dealers come to be imaged, in my mind, as the monkeys who make ropes of the pictures, to swing by. Then, every now and then at some old stable, or wine-cellar, or timber-shed, behind some forgotten vats or faggots, somebody finds a fresco of Perugino's or Giotto's, but doesn't think much of it, and has no idea of having people coming into his cellar, or being obliged to move his faggots; and so he whitewashes the fresco, and puts the faggots back again; and these kind of persons, therefore, come generally to be imaged, in my mind, as the monkeys who taste the pictures, and spit them out, not finding them nice. While, finally, the squabbling for nuts and apples (called in Italy "bella liberta") goes on all day long.

86. Now, all this might soon be put an end to, if we English, who are so fond of travelling in the body, would also travel a little in soul! We think it a great triumph to get our packages and our persons carried at a fast pace, but we never take the slightest trouble to put any pace into our perceptions; we stay usually at home in thought, or if we ever mentally see the world, it is at the old stage-coach or waggon rate. Do but consider what an odd sight it would be, if it were only quite clear to you how things are really going on--how, here in England, we are making enormous and expensive efforts to produce new art of all kinds, knowing and confessing all the while that the greater part of it is bad, but struggling still to produce new patterns of wall-papers, and new shapes of teapots, and new pictures, and statues, and architecture; and pluming and cackling if ever a teapot or a picture has the least

good in it;--all the while taking no thought whatever of the best possible pictures, and statues, and wall-patterns already in existence, which require nothing but to be taken common care of, and kept from damp and dust: but we let the walls fall that Giotto patterned, and the canvases rot that Tintoret painted, and the architecture be dashed to pieces that St. Louis built, while we are furnishing our drawing-rooms with prize upholstery, and writing accounts of our handsome warehouses to the country papers. Don't think I use my words vaguely or generally: I speak of literal facts. Giotto's frescoes at Assisi are perishing at this moment for want of decent care; Tintoret's pictures in San Sebastian, at Venice, are at this instant rotting piecemeal into grey rags; St. Louis's chapel, at Carcassonne, is at this moment lying in shattered fragments in the market-place. And here we are all cawing and crowing, poor little half-fledged daws as we are, about the pretty sticks and wool in our own nests. There's hardly a day passes, when I am at home, but I get a letter from some well-meaning country clergyman, deeply anxious about the state of his parish church, and breaking his heart to get money together that he may hold up some wretched remnant of Tudor tracery, with one niche in the corner and no statue-- when all the while the mightiest piles of religious architecture and sculpture that ever the world saw are being blasted and withered away, without one glance of pity or regret. The country clergyman does not care for *them*--he has a sea-sick imagination that cannot cross channel. What is it to him, if the angels of Assisi fade from its vaults, or the queens and kings of Chartres fall from their pedestals? They are not in his parish.

87. "What!" you will say, "are we not to produce any new art, nor take care of our parish churches?" No, certainly not, until you have taken proper care of the art you have got already, and of the best churches out of the parish. Your first and proper standing is not as churchwardens and parish overseers, in an English county, but as members of the great Christian community of Europe. And as members of that community (in which alone, observe, pure and precious ancient art exists, for there is none in America, none in Asia, none in Africa), you conduct yourselves precisely as a manufacturer would, who attended to his looms, but left his warehouse without a roof. The rain floods your warehouse, the rats frolic in it, the spiders spin in it, the choughs build in it, the wall-plague frets and festers in it; and still you keep weave, weave, weaving at your wretched webs, and thinking you are

growing rich, while more is gnawed out of your warehouse in an hour than you can weave in a twelvemonth.

88. Even this similitude is not absurd enough to set us rightly forth. The weaver would, or might, at least, hope that his new woof was as stout as the old ones, and that, therefore, in spite of rain and ravage, he would have something to wrap himself in when he needed it. But *our* webs rot as we spin. The very fact that we despise the great art of the past shows that we cannot produce great art now. If we could do it, we should love it when we saw it done--if we really cared for it, we should recognize it and keep it; but we don't care for it. It is not art that we want; it is amusement, gratification of pride, present gain--anything in the world but art: let it rot, we shall always have enough to talk about and hang over our sideboards.

89. You will (I hope) finally ask me what is the outcome of all this, practicable tomorrow morning by us who are sitting here? These are the main practical outcomes of it: In the first place, don't grumble when you hear of a new picture being bought by Government at a large price. There are many pictures in Europe now in danger of destruction which are, in the true sense of the word, priceless; the proper price is simply that which it is necessary to give to get and to save them. If you can get them for fifty pounds, do; if not for less than a hundred, do; if not for less than five thousand, do; if not for less than twenty thousand, do; never mind being imposed upon: there is nothing disgraceful in being imposed upon; the only disgrace is in imposing; and you can't in general get anything much worth having, in the way of Continental art, but it must be with the help or connivance of numbers of people who, indeed, ought to have nothing to do with the matter, but who practically have, and always will have, everything to do with it; and if you don't choose to submit to be cheated by them out of a ducat here and a zecchin there, you will be cheated by them out of your picture; and whether you are most imposed upon in losing that, or the zecchins, I think I may leave you to judge; though I know there are many political economists, who would rather leave a bag of gold on a garret-table, than give a porter sixpence extra to carry it downstairs.

That, then, is the first practical outcome of the matter. Never grumble, but be glad when you hear of a new picture being bought at a large price. In the long run, the dearest pictures are always the best bargains; and, I repeat, (for else you might think I said it in mere hurry of talk, and not deliberately,) there are some pictures

which are without price. You should stand, nationally, at the edge of Dover cliffs--
Shakespeare's--and wave blank cheques in the eyes of the nations on the other side
of the sea, freely offered, for such and such canvases of theirs.

90. Then the next practical outcome of it is--Never buy a copy of a picture,
under any circumstances whatever. All copies are bad; because no painter who is
worth a straw ever *will* copy. He will make a study of a picture he likes, for his
own use, in his own way; but he won't and can't copy. Whenever you buy a copy,
you buy so much misunderstanding of the original, and encourage a dull person in
following a business he is not fit for, besides increasing ultimately chances of mistake and imposture, and farthering, as directly as money *can* farther, the cause of
ignorance in all directions. You may, in fact, consider yourself as having purchased
a certain quantity of mistakes; and, according to your power, being engaged in dis-
seminating them.

91. I do not mean, however, that copies should never be made. A certain number of dull persons should always be employed by a Government in making the
most accurate copies possible of all good pictures; these copies, though artistically
valueless, would be historically and documentarily valuable, in the event of the
destruction of the original picture. The studies also made by great artists for their
own use, should be sought after with the greatest eagerness; they are often to be
bought cheap; and in connection with the mechanical copies, would become very
precious: tracings from frescoes and other large works are also of great value; for
though a tracing is liable to just as many mistakes as a copy, the mistakes in a tracing are of one kind only, which may be allowed for, but the mistakes of a common
copyist are of all conceivable kinds: finally, engravings, in so far as they convey
certain facts about the pictures, without pretending adequately to represent or give
an idea of the pictures, are often serviceable and valuable. I can't, of course, enter
into details in these matters just now; only this main piece of advice I can safely give
you--never to buy copies of pictures (for your private possession) which pretend to
give a facsimile that shall be in any wise representative of, or equal to, the original.
Whenever you do so, you are only lowering your taste, and wasting your money.
And if you are generous and wise, you will be ready rather to subscribe as much
as you would have given for a copy of a great picture towards its purchase, or the
purchase of some other like it, by the nation. There ought to be a great National So-

ciety instituted for the purchase of pictures; presenting them to the various galleries in our great cities, and watching there over their safety: but in the meantime, you can always act safely and beneficially by merely allowing your artist friends to buy pictures for you, when they see good ones. Never buy for yourselves, nor go to the foreign dealers; but let any painter whom you know be entrusted, when he finds a neglected old picture in an old house, to try if he cannot get it for you; then, if you like it, keep it; if not, send it to the hammer, and you will find that you do not lose money on pictures so purchased.

92. And the third and chief practical outcome of the matter is this general one: Wherever you go, whatever you do, act more for **preservation** and less for **production**. I assure you, the world is, generally speaking, in calamitous disorder, and just because you have managed to thrust some of the lumber aside, and get an available corner for yourselves, you think you should do nothing but sit spinning in it all day long--while, as householders and economists, your first thought and effort should be, to set things more square all about you. Try to set the ground floors in order, and get the rottenness out of your granaries. **Then** sit and spin, but not till then.

93. IV. DISTRIBUTION.--And now, lastly, we come to the fourth great head of our inquiry, the question of the wise distribution of the art we have gathered and preserved. It must be evident to us, at a moment's thought, that the way in which works of art are on the whole most useful to the nation to which they belong, must be by their collection in public galleries, supposing those galleries properly managed. But there is one disadvantage attached necessarily to gallery exhibition-- namely, the extent of mischief which may be done by one foolish curator. As long as the pictures which form the national wealth are disposed in private collections, the chance is always that the people who buy them will be just the people who are fond of them; and that the sense of exchangeable value in the commodity they possess, will induce them, even if they do not esteem it themselves, to take such care of it as will preserve its value undiminished. At all events, so long as works of art are scattered through the nation, no universal destruction of them is possible; a certain average only are lost by accidents from time to time. But when they are once collected in a large public gallery, if the appointment of curator becomes in any way a matter of formality, or the post is so lucrative as to be disputed by place-hunters, let but one foolish or careless person get possession of it, and perhaps you may have

all your fine pictures repainted, and the national property destroyed, in a month. That is actually the case at this moment, in several great foreign galleries. They are the places of execution of pictures: over their doors you only want the Dantesque inscription, "Lasciate ogni speranza, voi che entrate."

94. Supposing, however, this danger properly guarded against, as it would be always by a nation which either knew the value, or understood the meaning, of painting,[12] arrangement in a public gallery is the safest, as well as the most serviceable, method of exhibiting pictures; and it is the only mode in which their historical value can be brought out, and their historical meaning made clear. But great good is also to be done by encouraging the private possession of pictures; partly as a means of study, (much more being always discovered in any work of art by a person who has it perpetually near him than by one who only sees it from time to time,) and also as a means of refining the habits and touching the hearts of the masses of the nation in their domestic life.

> [Note 12: It would be a great point gained towards the preservation of pictures if it were made a rule that at every operation they underwent, the exact spots in which they have been repainted should be recorded in writing.]

95. For these last purposes, the most serviceable art is the living art of the time; the particular tastes of the people will be best met, and their particular ignorances best corrected, by painters labouring in the midst of them, more or less guided to the knowledge of what is wanted by the degree of sympathy with which their work is received. So then, generally, it should be the object of government, and of all patrons of art, to collect, as far as may be, the works of dead masters in public galleries, arranging them so as to illustrate the history of nations, and the progress and influence of their arts; and to encourage the private possession of the works of *living* masters. And the first and best way in which to encourage such private possession is, of course, to keep down the prices of them as far as you can.

I hope there are not a great many painters in the room; if there are, I entreat their patience for the next quarter of an hour: if they will bear with me for so long, I hope they will not, finally, be offended by what I am going to say.

96. I repeat, trusting to their indulgence in the interim, that the first object of our national economy, as respects the distribution of modern art, should be steadily

and rationally to limit its prices, since by doing so, you will produce two effects: you will make the painters produce more pictures, two or three instead of one, if they wish to make money; and you will, by bringing good pictures within the reach of people of moderate income, excite the general interest of the nation in them, increase a thousandfold the demand for the commodity, and therefore its wholesome and natural production.

97. I know how many objections must arise in your minds at this moment to what I say; but you must be aware that it is not possible for me in an hour to explain all the moral and commercial bearings of such a principle as this. Only, believe me, I do not speak lightly; I think I have considered all the objections which could be rationally brought forward, though I have time at present only to glance at the main one--namely, the idea that the high prices paid for modern pictures are either honourable, or serviceable, to the painter. So far from this being so, I believe one of the principal obstacles to the progress of modern art to be the high prices given for good modern pictures. For observe first the action of this high remuneration on the artist's mind. If he "gets on," as it is called, catches the eye of the public, and especially of the public of the upper classes, there is hardly any limit to the fortune he may acquire; so that, in his early years, his mind is naturally led to dwell on this worldly and wealthy eminence as the main thing to be reached by his art; if he finds that he is not gradually rising towards it, he thinks there is something wrong in his work; or, if he is too proud to think that, still the bribe of wealth and honour warps him from his honest labour into efforts to attract attention; and he gradually loses both his power of mind and his rectitude of purpose. This, according to the degree of avarice or ambition which exists in any painter's mind, is the necessary influence upon him of the hope of great wealth and reputation. But the harm is still greater, in so far as the possibility of attaining fortune of this kind tempts people continually to become painters who have no real gift for the work; and on whom these motives of mere worldly interest have exclusive influence;--men who torment and abuse the patient workers, eclipse or thrust aside all delicate and good pictures by their own gaudy and coarse ones, corrupt the taste of the public, and do the greatest amount of mischief to the schools of art in their day which it is possible for their capacities to effect; and it is quite wonderful how much mischief may be done even by small capacity. If you could by any means succeed in keeping the prices of pictures down,

you would throw all these disturbers out of the way at once.

98. You may perhaps think that this severe treatment would do more harm than good, by withdrawing the wholesome element of emulation, and giving no stimulus to exertion; but I am sorry to say that artists will always be sufficiently jealous of one another, whether you pay them large or low prices; and as for stimulus to exertion, believe me, no good work in this world was ever done for money, nor while the slightest thought of money affected the painter's mind. Whatever idea of pecuniary value enters into his thoughts as he works, will, in proportion to the distinctness of its presence, shorten his power. A real painter will work for you exquisitely, if you give him, as I told you a little while ago, bread and water and salt; and a bad painter will work badly and hastily, though you give him a palace to live in, and a princedom to live upon. Turner got, in his earlier years, half a crown a day and his supper (not bad pay, neither); and he learned to paint upon that. And I believe that there is no chance of art's truly flourishing in any country, until you make it a simple and plain business, providing its masters with an easy competence, but rarely with anything more. And I say this, not because I despise the great painter, but because I honour him; and I should no more think of adding to his respectability or happiness by giving him riches, than, if Shakespeare or Milton were alive, I should think we added to *their* respectability, or were likely to get better work from them, by making them millionaires.

99. But, observe, it is not only the painter himself whom you injure, by giving him too high prices; you injure all the inferior painters of the day. If they are modest, they will be discouraged and depressed by the feeling that their doings are worth so little, comparatively, in your eyes;--if proud, all their worst passions will be aroused, and the insult or opprobrium which they will try to cast on their successful rival will not only afflict and wound him, but at last sour and harden him: he cannot pass through such a trial without grievous harm.

100. That, then, is the effect you produce on the painter of mark, and on the inferior ones of his own standing. But you do worse than this; you deprive yourselves, by what you give for the fashionable picture, of the power of helping the younger men who are coming forward. Be it admitted, for argument's sake, if you are not convinced by what I have said, that you do no harm to the great man by paying him well; yet certainly you do him no special good. His reputation is established, and

his fortune made; he does not care whether you buy or not; he thinks he is rather doing you a favour than otherwise by letting you have one of his pictures at all. All the good you do him is to help him to buy a new pair of carriage horses; whereas, with that same sum which thus you cast away, you might have relieved the hearts and preserved the health of twenty young painters; and if, among those twenty, you but chanced on one in whom a true latent power had been hindered by his poverty, just consider what a far-branching, far-embracing good you have wrought with that lucky expenditure of yours. I say, "Consider it," in vain; you cannot consider it, for you cannot conceive the sickness of heart with which a young painter of deep feeling toils through his first obscurity;--his sense of the strong voice within him, which you will not hear;--his vain, fond, wondering witness to the things you will not see;--his far-away perception of things that he could accomplish if he had but peace, and time, all unapproachable and vanishing from him, because no one will leave him peace or grant him time: all his friends falling back from him; those whom he would most reverently obey rebuking and paralysing him; and, last and worst of all, those who believe in him the most faithfully suffering by him the most bitterly;--the wife's eyes, in their sweet ambition, shining brighter as the cheek wastes away; and the little lips at his side parched and pale, which one day, he knows, though he may never see it, will quiver so proudly when they call his name, calling him "our father." You deprive yourselves, by your large expenditure for pictures of mark, of the power of relieving and redeeming *this* distress; you injure the painter whom you pay so largely;--and what, after all, have you done for yourselves or got for yourselves? It does not in the least follow that the hurried work of a fashionable painter will contain more for your money than the quiet work of some unknown man. In all probability, you will find, if you rashly purchase what is popular at a high price, that you have got one picture you don't care for, for a sum which would have bought twenty you would have delighted in.

101. For remember always, that the price of a picture by a living artist never represents, never *can* represent, the quantity of labour or value in it. Its price represents, for the most part, the degree of desire which the rich people of the country have to possess it. Once get the wealthy classes to imagine that the possession of pictures by a given artist adds to their "gentility," and there is no price which his work may not immediately reach, and for years maintain; and in buying at that

price, you are not getting value for your money, but merely disputing for victory in a contest of ostentation. And it is hardly possible to spend your money in a worse or more wasteful way; for though you may not be doing it for ostentation yourself, you are, by your pertinacity, nourishing the ostentation of others; you meet them in their game of wealth, and continue it for them; if they had not found an opposite player, the game would have been done; for a proud man can find no enjoyment in possessing himself of what nobody disputes with him. So that by every farthing you give for a picture beyond its fair price--that is to say, the price which will pay the painter for his time--you are not only cheating yourself and buying vanity, but you are stimulating the vanity of others; paying, literally, for the cultivation of pride. You may consider every pound that you spend above the just price of a work of art, as an investment in a cargo of mental quick-lime or guano, which, being laid on the fields of human nature, is to grow a harvest of pride. You are in fact ploughing and harrowing, in a most valuable part of your land, in order to reap the whirlwind; you are setting your hand stoutly to Job's agriculture--"Let thistles grow instead of wheat, and cockle instead of barley."

102. Well, but you will say, there is one advantage in high prices, which more than counter-balances all this mischief, namely, that by great reward we both urge and enable a painter to produce rather one perfect picture than many inferior ones: and one perfect picture (so you tell us, and we believe it) is worth a great number of inferior ones.

It is so; but you cannot get it by paying for it. A great work is only done when the painter gets into the humour for it, likes his subject, and determines to paint it as well as he can, whether he is paid for it or not; but bad work, and generally the worst sort of bad work, is done when he is trying to produce a showy picture, or one that shall appear to have as much labour in it as shall be worth a high price.[13]

[Note 13: When this lecture was delivered, I gave here some data for approximate estimates of the average value of good modern pictures of different classes; but the subject is too complicated to be adequately treated in writing, without introducing more detail than the reader will have patience for. But I may state, roughly, that prices above a hundred guineas are in general extravagant for water-colours, and above five hundred for oils. An artist almost always does wrong who puts more work than these prices will remunerate him for into any single canvas--his talent would be better employed in painting two pictures than one so elaborate. The water-colour painters also are getting into the habit of making their drawings too large, and in a measure attaching their price rather to breadth and extent of touch than to thoughtful labour. Of course marked exceptions occur here and there, as in the case of John Lewis, whose drawings are wrought with unfailing precision throughout, whatever their scale. Hardly any price can be remunerative for such work.]

103. There is, however, another point, and a still more important one, bearing on this matter of purchase, than the keeping down of prices to a rational standard. And that is, that you pay your prices into the hands of living men, and do not pour them into coffins.

For observe that, as we arrange our payment of pictures at present, no artist's work is worth half its proper value while he is alive. The moment he dies, his pictures, if they are good, reach double their former value; but, that rise of price represents simply a profit made by the intelligent dealer or purchaser on his past purchases. So that the real facts of the matter are, that the British public, spending a certain sum annually in art, determines that, of every thousand it pays, only five hundred shall go to the painter, or shall be at all concerned in the production of art; and that the other five hundred shall be paid merely as a testimonial to the intelligent dealer, who knew what to buy. Now, testimonials are very pretty and proper things, within due limits; but testimonial to the amount of a hundred per cent. on the total expenditure is not good political economy. Do not, therefore, in general, unless you see it to be necessary for its preservation, buy the picture of a dead artist. If you fear that it may be exposed to contempt or neglect, buy it; its price will then, probably, not be high: if you want to put it into a public gallery, buy it; you are sure, then, that you do not spend your money selfishly: or, if you loved the man's work while he was alive, and bought it then, buy it also now, if you can see no living work equal to it. But if you did not buy it while the man was living, never buy it after he is dead: you are then doing no good to him, and you are doing some shame to yourself. Look around you for pictures that you really like, and in buying which you can help some genius yet unperished--that is the best atonement you can make to the one you have neglected--and give to the living and struggling painter at once wages, and testimonial.

104. So far then of the motives which should induce us to keep down the prices of modern art, and thus render it, as a private possession, attainable by greater numbers of people than at present. But we should strive to render it accessible to them in other ways also--chiefly by the permanent decoration of public buildings; and it is in this field that I think we may look for the profitable means of providing that constant employment for young painters of which we were speaking last evening.

The first and most important kind of public buildings which we are always sure to want, are schools: and I would ask you to consider very carefully, whether we may not wisely introduce some great changes in the way of school decoration. Hitherto, as far as I know, it has either been so difficult to give all the education we wanted to our lads, that we have been obliged to do it, if at all, with cheap furniture and bare walls; or else we have considered that cheap furniture and bare walls are a proper part of the means of education; and supposed that boys learned best when they sat on hard forms, and had nothing but blank plaster about and above them whereupon to employ their spare attention; also, that it was as well they should be accustomed to rough and ugly conditions of things, partly by way of preparing them for the hardships of life, and partly that there might be the least possible damage done to floors and forms, in the event of their becoming, during the master's absence, the fields or instruments of battle. All this is so far well and necessary, as it relates to the training of country lads, and the first training of boys in general. But there certainly comes a period in the life of a well-educated youth, in which one of the principal elements of his education is, or ought to be, to give him refinement of habits; and not only to teach him the strong exercises of which his frame is capable, but also to increase his bodily sensibility and refinement, and show him such small matters as the way of handling things properly, and treating them considerately.

105. Not only so; but I believe the notion of fixing the attention by keeping the room empty, is a wholly mistaken one: I think it is just in the emptiest room that the mind wanders most; for it gets restless, like a bird, for want of a perch, and casts about for any possible means of getting out and away. And even if it be fixed, by an effort, on the business in hand, that business becomes itself repulsive, more than it need be, by the vileness of its associations; and many a study appears dull or painful to a boy, when it is pursued on a blotted deal desk, under a wall with nothing on it but scratches and pegs, which would have been pursued pleasantly enough

in a curtained corner of his father's library, or at the lattice window of his cottage. Now, my own belief is, that the best study of all is the most beautiful; and that a quiet glade of forest, or the nook of a lake shore, are worth all the schoolrooms in Christendom, when once you are past the multiplication table; but be that as it may, there is no question at all but that a time ought to come in the life of a well-trained youth, when he can sit at a writing-table without wanting to throw the inkstand at his neighbour; and when also he will feel more capable of certain efforts of mind with beautiful and refined forms about him than with ugly ones. When that time comes, he ought to be advanced into the decorated schools; and this advance ought to be one of the important and honourable epochs of his life.

106. I have not time, however, to insist on the mere serviceableness to our youth of refined architectural decoration, as such; for I want you to consider the probable influence of the particular kind of decoration which I wish you to get for them, namely, historical painting. You know we have hitherto been in the habit of conveying all our historical knowledge, such as it is, by the ear only, never by the eye; all our notion of things being ostensibly derived from verbal description, not from sight. Now, I have no doubt that, as we grow gradually wiser--and we are doing so every day--we shall discover at last that the eye is a nobler organ than the ear; and that through the eye we must, in reality, obtain, or put into form, nearly all the useful information we are to have about this world. Even as the matter stands, you will find that the knowledge which a boy is supposed to receive from verbal description is only available to him so far as in any underhand way he gets a sight of the thing you are talking about. I remember well that, for many years of my life, the only notion I had of the look of a Greek knight was complicated between recollection of a small engraving in my pocket Pope's Homer, and reverent study of the Horse Guards. And though I believe that most boys collect their ideas from more varied sources and arrange them more carefully than I did; still, whatever sources they seek must always be ocular: if they are clever boys, they will go and look at the Greek vases and sculptures in the British Museum, and at the weapons in our armouries--they will see what real armour is like in lustre, and what Greek armour was like in form, and so put a fairly true image together, but still not, in ordinary cases, a very living or interesting one.

107. Now, the use of your decorative painting would be, in myriads of ways,

to animate their history for them, and to put the living aspect of past things before their eyes as faithfully as intelligent invention can; so that the master shall have nothing to do but once to point to the schoolroom walls, and for ever afterwards the meaning of any word would be fixed in a boy's mind in the best possible way. Is it a question of classical dress--what a tunic was like, or a chlamys, or a peplus? At this day, you have to point to some vile woodcut, in the middle of a dictionary page, representing the thing hung upon a stick; but then, you would point to a hundred figures, wearing the actual dress, in its fiery colours, in all actions of various stateliness or strength; you would understand at once how it fell round the people's limbs as they stood, how it drifted from their shoulders as they went, how it veiled their faces as they wept, how it covered their heads in the day of battle. *Now*, if you want to see what a weapon is like, you refer, in like manner, to a numbered page, in which there are spear-heads in rows, and sword-hilts in symmetrical groups; and gradually the boy gets a dim mathematical notion how one scimitar is hooked to the right and another to the left, and one javelin has a knob to it and another none: while one glance at your good picture would show him,--and the first rainy afternoon in the schoolroom would for ever fix in his mind,--the look of the sword and spear as they fell or flew; and how they pierced, or bent, or shattered--how men wielded them, and how men died by them.

108. But far more than all this, is it a question not of clothes or weapons, but of men? how can we sufficiently estimate the effect on the mind of a noble youth, at the time when the world opens to him, of having faithful and touching representations put before him of the acts and presences of great men--how many a resolution, which would alter and exalt the whole course of his after-life, might be formed, when in some dreamy twilight he met, through his own tears, the fixed eyes of those shadows of the great dead, unescapable and calm, piercing to his soul; or fancied that their lips moved in dread reproof or soundless exhortation? And if but for one out of many this were true--if yet, in a few, you could be sure that such influence had indeed changed their thoughts and destinies, and turned the eager and reckless youth, who would have cast away his energies on the race-horse or the gambling-table, to that noble life-race, that holy life-hazard, which should win all glory to himself and all good to his country,--would not that, to some purpose, be "political economy of art"?

109. And observe, there could be no monotony, no exhaustibleness, in the scenes required to be thus portrayed. Even if there were, and you wanted for every school in the kingdom, one death of Leonidas; one battle of Marathon; one death of Cleobis and Bito; there need not therefore be more monotony in your art than there was in the repetition of a given cycle of subjects by the religious painters of Italy. But we ought not to admit a cycle at all. For though we had as many great schools as we have great cities (one day I hope we *shall* have), centuries of painting would not exhaust, in all the number of them, the noble and pathetic subjects which might be chosen from the history of even one noble nation. But, beside this, you will not, in a little while, limit your youths' studies to so narrow fields as you do now. There will come a time--I am sure of it--when it will be found that the same practical results, both in mental discipline and in political philosophy, are to be attained by the accurate study of mediaeval and modern as of ancient history; and that the facts of mediaeval and modern history are, on the whole, the most important to us. And among these noble groups of constellated schools which I foresee arising in our England, I foresee also that there will be divided fields of thought; and that while each will give its scholars a great general idea of the world's history, such as all men should possess--each will also take upon itself, as its own special duty, the closer study of the course of events in some given place or time. It will review the rest of history, but it will exhaust its own special field of it; and found its moral and political teaching on the most perfect possible analysis of the results of human conduct in one place, and at one epoch. And then, the galleries of that school will be painted with the historical scenes belonging to the age which it has chosen for its special study.

110. So far, then, of art as you may apply it to that great series of public buildings which you devote to the education of youth. The next large class of public buildings in which we should introduce it, is one which I think a few years more of national progress will render more serviceable to us than they have been lately. I mean, buildings for the meetings of guilds of trades.

And here, for the last time, I must again interrupt the course of our chief inquiry, in order to state one other principle of political economy, which is perfectly simple and indisputable; but which, nevertheless, we continually get into commercial embarrassments for want of understanding; and not only so, but suffer much hindrance in our commercial discoveries, because many of our business men do not practically admit it.

Supposing half a dozen or a dozen men were cast ashore from a wreck on an uninhabited island, and left to their own resources, one of course, according to his capacity, would be set to one business and one to another; the strongest to dig and cut wood, and to build huts for the rest: the most dexterous to make shoes out of bark and coats out of skins; the best educated to look for iron or lead in the rocks, and to plan the channels for the irrigation of the fields. But though their labours were thus naturally severed, that small group of shipwrecked men would understand well enough that the speediest progress was to be made by helping each other,--not by opposing each other: and they would know that this help could only be properly given so long as they were frank and open in their relations, and the difficulties which each lay under properly explained to the rest. So that any appearance of secrecy or separateness in the actions of any of them would instantly, and justly, be looked upon with suspicion by the rest, as the sign of some selfish or foolish proceeding on the part of the individual. If, for instance, the scientific man were found to have gone out at night, unknown to the rest, to alter the sluices, the others would think, and in all probability rightly think, that he wanted to get the best supply of water to his own field; and if the shoemaker refused to show them where the bark grew which he made the sandals of, they would naturally think, and in all probability rightly think, that he didn't want them to see how much there was of it, and that he meant to ask from them more corn and potatoes in exchange for his sandals than the trouble of making them deserved. And thus, although each man would have a portion of time to himself in which he was allowed to do what he chose without let or inquiry,--so long as he was working in that particular business which he had undertaken for the common benefit, any secrecy on his part would be immediately supposed to mean mischief; and would require to be accounted for, or put an end to: and this all the more because whatever the work might be, certainly there would be difficulties about it which, when once they were well explained, might be more or less done away with by the help of the rest; so that assuredly every one of them would advance with his labour not only more happily, but more profitably and quickly, by having no secrets, and by frankly bestowing, and frankly receiving, such help as lay in his way to get or to give.

111. And, just as the best and richest result of wealth and happiness to the whole of them would follow on their perseverance in such a system of frank communication and of helpful labour;--so precisely the worst and poorest result would be obtained by a system of secrecy and of enmity; and each man's happiness and wealth would assuredly be diminished in proportion to the degree in which jealousy and concealment became their social and economical principles. It would not, in the long run, bring good, but only evil, to the man of science, if, instead of telling openly where he had found good iron, he carefully concealed every new bed of it, that he might ask, in exchange for the rare ploughshare, more corn from the farmer, or, in exchange for the rude needle, more labour from the sempstress: and it would not ultimately bring good, but only evil, to the farmers, if they sought to burn each other's cornstacks, that they might raise the value of their grain, or if the sempstresses tried to break each other's needles, that each might get all the stitching to herself.

112. Now, these laws of human action are precisely as authoritative in their application to the conduct of a million of men, as to that of six or twelve. All enmity, jealousy, opposition, and secrecy are wholly, and in all circumstances, destructive in their nature--not productive; and all kindness, fellowship, and communicativeness are invariably productive in their operation,--not destructive; and the evil principles of opposition and exclusiveness are not rendered less fatal, but more fatal, by their acceptance among large masses of men; more fatal, I say, exactly in proportion as their influence is more secret. For though the opposition does always its own simple, necessary, direct quantity of harm, and withdraws always its own simple, necessary, measurable quantity of wealth from the sum possessed by the community, yet, in proportion to the size of the community, it does another and more refined mischief than this, by concealing its own fatality under aspects of mercantile complication and expediency, and giving rise to multitudes of false theories based on a mean belief in narrow and immediate appearances of good done here and there by things which have the universal and everlasting nature of evil. So that the time and powers of the nation are wasted, not only in wretched struggling against each other, but in vain complaints, and groundless discouragements, and empty investigations, and useless experiments in laws, and elections, and inventions; with hope always to pull wisdom through some new-shaped slit in a ballot-box, and to drag

prosperity down out of the clouds along some new knot of electric wire; while all the while Wisdom stands calling at the corners of the streets, and the blessing of Heaven waits ready to rain down upon us, deeper than the rivers and broader than the dew, if only we will obey the first plain principles of humanity, and the first plain precepts of the skies: "Execute true judgment, and show mercy and compassion, every man to his brother; and let none of you imagine evil against his brother in your heart."[14]

> [Note 14: It would be well if, instead of preaching continually about the doctrine of faith and good works, our clergymen would simply explain to their people a little what good works mean. There is not a chapter in all the book we profess to believe, more specially and directly written for England than the second of Habakkuk, and I never in all my life heard one of its practical texts preached from. I suppose the clergymen are all afraid, and know their flocks, while they will sit quite politely to hear syllogisms out of the epistle to the Romans, would get restive directly if they ever pressed a practical text home to them. But we should have no mercantile catastrophes, and no distressful pauperism, if we only read often, and took to heart, those plain words:--"Yea, also, because he is a proud man, neither keepeth at home, who enlargeth his desire as hell, and cannot be satisfied,--Shall not all these take up a parable against him, and a taunting proverb against him, and say, 'Woe to him that increaseth that which is not his: and to him that ***ladeth himself with thick clay***'?" (What a glorious history in one metaphor, of the life of a man greedy of fortune!) "Woe to him that coveteth an evil covetousness that he may set his nest on high. Woe to him that buildeth a town with blood, and establisheth a city by iniquity. Behold, is it not of the Lord of Hosts that the people shall labour in the very fire, and the people shall weary themselves for very vanity?"

> The Americans, who have been sending out ships with sham bolt-heads on their timbers, and only half their bolts, may meditate on that "buildeth a town with blood."]

113. Therefore, I believe most firmly, that as the laws of national prosperity get familiar to us, we shall more and more cast our toil into social and communicative systems; and that one of the first means of our doing so, will be the re-establishing guilds of every important trade in a vital, not formal, condition;--that there will

be a great council or government house for the members of every trade, built in whatever town of the kingdom occupies itself principally in such trade, with minor council-halls in other cities; and to each council-hall, officers attached, whose first business may be to examine into the circumstances of every operative, in that trade, who chooses to report himself to them when out of work, and to set him to work, if he is indeed able and willing, at a fixed rate of wages, determined at regular periods in the council-meetings; and whose next duty may be to bring reports before the council of all improvements made in the business, and means of its extension: not allowing private patents of any kind, but making all improvements available to every member of the guild, only allotting, after successful trial of them, a certain reward to the inventors.

114. For these, and many other such purposes, such halls will be again, I trust, fully established, and then, in the paintings and decorations of them, especial effort ought to be made to express the worthiness and honourableness of the trade for whose members they are founded. For I believe one of the worst symptoms of modern society to be, its notion of great inferiority, and ungentlemanliness, as necessarily belonging to the character of a tradesman. I believe tradesmen may be, ought to be--often are, more gentlemen than idle and useless people: and I believe that art may do noble work by recording in the hall of each trade, the services which men belonging to that trade have done for their country, both preserving the portraits, and recording the important incidents in the lives, of those who have made great advances in commerce and civilization. I cannot follow out this subject--it branches too far, and in too many directions; besides, I have no doubt you will at once see and accept the truth of the main principle, and be able to think it out for yourselves. I would fain also have said something of what might be done, in the same manner, for almshouses and hospitals, and for what, as I shall try to explain in notes to this lecture, we may hope to see, some day, established with a different meaning in their name than that they now bear--work-houses; but I have detained you too long already, and cannot permit myself to trespass further on your patience except only to recapitulate, in closing, the simple principles respecting wealth which we have gathered during the course of our inquiry; principles which are nothing more than the literal and practical acceptance of the saying which is in all good men's mouths--namely, that they are stewards or ministers of whatever talents are entrusted to

them.

115. Only, is it not a strange thing, that while we more or less accept the meaning of that saying, so long as it is considered metaphorical, we never accept its meaning in its own terms? You know the lesson is given us under the form of a story about money. Money was given to the servants to make use of: the unprofitable servant dug in the earth, and hid his lord's money. Well, we, in our political and spiritual application of this, say, that of course money doesn't mean money: it means wit, it means intellect, it means influence in high quarters, it means everything in the world except itself. And do not you see what a pretty and pleasant come-off there is for most of us, in this spiritual application? Of course, if we had wit, we would use it for the good of our fellow-creatures. But we haven't wit. Of course, if we had influence with the bishops, we would use it for the good of the Church; but we haven't any influence with the bishops. Of course, if we had political power, we would use it for the good of the nation; but we have no political power; we have no talents entrusted to us of any sort or kind. It is true we have a little money, but the parable can't possibly mean anything so vulgar as money; our money's our own.

116. I believe, if you think seriously of this matter, you will feel that the first and most literal application is just as necessary a one as any other--that the story does very specially mean what it says--plain money; and that the reason we don't at once believe it does so, is a sort of tacit idea that while thought, wit, and intellect, and all power of birth and position, are indeed ***given*** to us, and, therefore, to be laid out for the Giver--our wealth has not been given to us; but we have worked for it, and have a right to spend it as we choose. I think you will find that is the real substance of our understanding in this matter. Beauty, we say, is given by God--it is a talent; strength is given by God--it is a talent; position is given by God--it is a talent; but money is proper wages for our day's work--it is not a talent, it is a due. We may justly spend it on ourselves, if we have worked for it.

117. And there would be some shadow of excuse for this, were it not that the very power of making the money is itself only one of the applications of that intellect or strength which we confess to be talents. Why is one man richer than another? Because he is more industrious, more persevering, and more sagacious. Well, who made him more persevering or more sagacious than others? That power of endurance, that quickness of apprehension, that calmness of judgment, which enable

him to seize the opportunities that others lose, and persist in the lines of conduct in which others fail--are these not talents?--are they not, in the present state of the world, among the most distinguished and influential of mental gifts? And is it not wonderful, that while we should be utterly ashamed to use a superiority of body, in order to thrust our weaker companions aside from some place of advantage, we unhesitatingly use our superiorities of mind to thrust them back from whatever good that strength of mind can attain? You would be indignant if you saw a strong man walk into a theatre or a lecture-room, and, calmly choosing the best place, take his feeble neighbour by the shoulder, and turn him out of it into the back seats, or the street. You would be equally indignant if you saw a stout fellow thrust himself up to a table where some hungry children were being fed, and reach his arm over their heads and take their bread from them. But you are not the least indignant if, when a man has stoutness of thought and swiftness of capacity, and, instead of being long-armed only, has the much greater gift of being long-headed--you think it perfectly just that he should use his intellect to take the bread out of the mouths of all the other men in the town who are of the same trade with him; or use his breadth and sweep of sight to gather some branch of the commerce of the country into one great cobweb, of which he is himself to be the central spider, making every thread vibrate with the points of his claws, and commanding every avenue with the facets of his eyes. You see no injustice in this.

118. But there is injustice; and, let us trust, one of which honourable men will at no very distant period disdain to be guilty. In some degree, however, it is indeed not unjust; in some degree, it is necessary and intended. It is assuredly just that idleness should be surpassed by energy; that the widest influence should be possessed by those who are best able to wield it; and that a wise man, at the end of his career, should be better off than a fool. But for that reason, is the fool to be wretched, utterly crushed down, and left in all the suffering which his conduct and capacity naturally inflict?--Not so. What do you suppose fools were made for? That you might tread upon them, and starve them, and get the better of them in every possible way? By no means. They were made that wise people might take care of them. That is the true and plain fact concerning the relations of every strong and wise man to the world about him. He has his strength given him, not that he may crush the weak, but that he may support and guide them. In his own household he

is to be the guide and the support of his children; out of his household he is still to be the father--that is, the guide and support--of the weak and the poor; not merely of the meritoriously weak and the innocently poor, but of the guiltily and punishably poor; of the men who ought to have known better--of the poor who ought to be ashamed of themselves. It is nothing to give pension and cottage to the widow who has lost her son; it is nothing to give food and medicine to the workman who has broken his arm, or the decrepit woman wasting in sickness. But it is something to use your time and strength to war with the waywardness and thoughtlessness of mankind; to keep the erring workman in your service till you have made him an unerring one; and to direct your fellow-merchant to the opportunity which his dulness would have lost. This is much; but it is yet more, when you have fully achieved the superiority which is due to you, and acquired the wealth which is the fitting reward of your sagacity, if you solemnly accept the responsibility of it, as it is the helm and guide of labour far and near.

119. For you who have it in your hands are in reality the pilots of the power and effort of the State. It is entrusted to you as an authority to be used for good or evil, just as completely as kingly authority was ever given to a prince, or military command to a captain. And, according to the quantity of it that you have in your hands, you are the arbiters of the will and work of England; and the whole issue, whether the work of the State shall suffice for the State or not, depends upon you. You may stretch out your sceptre over the heads of the English labourers, and say to them, as they stoop to its waving, "Subdue this obstacle that has baffled our fathers, put away this plague that consumes our children; water these dry places, plough these desert ones, carry this food to those who are in hunger; carry this light to those who are in darkness; carry this life to those who are in death;" or on the other side you may say to her labourers: "Here am I; this power is in my hand; come, build a mound here for me to be throned upon, high and wide; come, make crowns for my head, that men may see them shine from far away; come, weave tapestries for my feet, that I may tread softly on the silk and purple; come, dance before me, that I may be gay; and sing sweetly to me, that I may slumber; so shall I live in joy, and die in honour." And better than such an honourable death it were that the day had perished wherein we were born, and the night in which it was said there is a child conceived.

120. I trust that in a little while there will be few of our rich men who, through carelessness or covetousness, thus forfeit the glorious office which is intended for their hands. I said, just now, that wealth ill-used was as the net of the spider, entangling and destroying: but wealth well used is as the net of the sacred fisher who gathers souls of men out of the deep. A time will come--I do not think even now it is far from us--when this golden net of the world's wealth will be spread abroad as the flaming meshes of morning cloud are over the sky; bearing with them the joy of light and the dew of the morning, as well as the summons to honourable and peaceful toil. What less can we hope from your wealth than this, rich men of England, when once you feel fully how, by the strength of your possessions--not, observe, by the exhaustion, but by the administration of them and the power,--you can direct the acts--command the energies--inform the ignorance--prolong the existence, of the whole human race; and how, even of worldly wisdom, which man employs faithfully, it is true, not only that her ways are pleasantness, but that her paths are peace; and that, for all the children of men, as well as for those to whom she is given, Length of days is in her right hand, as in her left hand Riches and Honour?

ADDENDA

Note, p. 18.--"*Fatherly authority.*"

121. This statement could not, of course, be heard without displeasure by a certain class of politicians; and in one of the notices of these lectures given in the Manchester journals at the time, endeavour was made to get quit of it by referring to the Divine authority, as the only Paternal power with respect to which men were truly styled "brethren." Of course it is so, and, equally of course, all human government is nothing else than the executive expression of this Divine authority. The moment government ceases to be the practical enforcement of Divine law, it is tyranny; and the meaning which I attach to the words "paternal government," is, in more extended terms, simply this--"The executive fulfilment, by formal human methods, of the will of the Father of mankind respecting His children." I could not give such a definition of Government as this in a popular lecture; and even in written form, it will necessarily suggest many objections, of which I must notice and

answer the most probable.

Only, in order to avoid the recurrence of such tiresome phrases as "it may be answered in the second place," and "it will be objected in the third place," etc., I will ask the reader's leave to arrange the discussion in the form of simple dialogue, letting *O.* stand for objector, and *R.* for response.

122. *O.*--You define your paternal government to be the executive fulfilment, by formal human methods, of the Divine will. But, assuredly, that will cannot stand in need of aid or expression from human laws. It cannot fail of its fulfilment.

R. 122. In the final sense it cannot; and in that sense, men who are committing murder and stealing are fulfilling the will of God as much as the best and kindest people in the world. But in the limited and present sense, the only sense with which *we* have anything to do, God's will concerning man is fulfilled by some men, and thwarted by others. And those men who either persuade or enforce the doing of it, stand towards those who are rebellious against it exactly in the position of faithful children in a family, who, when the father is out of sight, either compel or persuade the rest to do as their father would have them, were he present; and in so far as they are expressing and maintaining, for the time, the paternal authority, they exercise, in the exact sense in which I mean the phrase to be understood, paternal government over the rest.

O.--But, if Providence has left a liberty to man in many things in order to prove him, why should human law abridge that liberty, and take upon itself to compel what the great Lawgiver does not compel?

123. *R.*--It is confessed, in the enactment of any law whatsoever, that human lawgivers have a right to do this. For, if you have no right to abridge any of the liberty which Providence has left to man, you have no right to punish any one for committing murder or robbery. You ought to leave them to the punishment of God and Nature. But if you think yourself under obligation to punish, as far as human laws can, the violation of the will of God by these great sins, you are certainly under the same obligation to punish, with proportionately less punishment, the violation of His will in less sins.

O.--No; you must not attempt to punish less sins by law, because you cannot properly define nor ascertain them. Everybody can determine whether murder has been committed or not, but you cannot determine how far people have been unjust or cruel in minor matters, and therefore cannot make or execute laws concerning minor matters.

R.--If I propose to you to punish faults which cannot be defined, or to execute laws which cannot be made equitable, reject the laws I propose. But do not generally object to the principle of law.

O.--Yes; I generally object to the principle of law as applied to minor things; because, if you could succeed (which you cannot) in regulating the entire conduct of men by law in little things as well as great, you would take away from human life all its probationary character, and render many virtues and pleasures impossible. You would reduce virtue to the movement of a machine, instead of the act of a spirit.

124. *R.*--You have just said, parenthetically, and I fully and willingly admit it, that it is impossible to regulate all minor matters by law. Is it not probable, therefore, that the degree in which it is *possible* to regulate them by it, is also the degree in which it is *right* to regulate them by it? Or what other means of judgment will you employ, to separate the things which ought to be formally regulated from the things which ought not? You admit that great sins should be legally repressed; but you say that small sins should not be legally repressed. How do you distinguish between great and small sins? and how do you intend to determine, or do you in practice of daily life determine, on what occasions you should compel people to do right, and on what occasions you should leave them the option of doing wrong?

O.--I think you cannot make any accurate or logical distinction in such matters; but that common sense and instinct have, in all civilised nations, indicated certain crimes of great social harmfulness, such as murder, theft, adultery, slander, and such like, which it is proper to repress legally; and that common sense and instinct indicate also the kind of crimes which it is proper for laws to let alone, such as miserliness, ill-natured speaking, and many of those commercial dishonesties which I have a notion you want your paternal government to interfere with.

R.--Pray do not alarm yourself about what my paternal government is likely to interfere with, but keep to the matter in hand. You say that "common sense and instinct" have, in all civilised nations, distinguished between the sins that ought to be legally dealt with and that ought not. Do you mean that the laws of all civilised nations are perfect?

O.--No; certainly not.

R.--Or that they are perfect at least in their discrimination of what crimes they should deal with, and what crimes they should let alone?

O.--No; not exactly.

R.--What *do* you mean, then?

125. *O.*--I mean that the general tendency is right in the laws of civilised nations; and that, in due course of time, natural sense and instinct point out the matters they should be brought to bear upon. And each question of legislation must be made a separate subject of inquiry as it presents itself: you cannot fix any general principles about what should be dealt with legally, and what should not.

R.--Supposing it to be so, do you think there are any points in which our English legislation is capable of amendment, as it bears on commercial and economical matters, in this present time?

O.--Of course I do.

R.--Well, then, let us discuss these together quietly; and if the points that I want amended seem to you incapable of amendment, or not in need of amendment, say so: but don't object, at starting, to the mere proposition of applying law to things which have not had law applied to them before. You have admitted the fitness of my expression, "paternal government": it only has been, and remains, a question between us, how far such government should extend. Perhaps you would like it only to regulate, among the children, the length of their lessons; and perhaps I should like it also to regulate the hardness of their cricket-balls: but cannot you wait quietly till you know what I want it to do, before quarrelling with the thing itself?

O.--No; I cannot wait quietly; in fact, I don't see any use in beginning such a discussion at all, because I am quite sure from the first, that you want to meddle with things that you have no business with, and to interfere with healthy liberty of action in all sorts of ways; and I know that you can't propose any laws that would be of real use.[15]

[Note 15: If the reader is displeased with me for putting this foolish speech into his mouth, I entreat his pardon; but he may be assured that it is a speech which would be made by many people, and the substance of which would be tacitly felt by many more, at this point of the discussion. I have really tried, up to this point, to make the objector as intelligent a person as it is possible for an author to imagine anybody to be who differs with him.]

126. *R.*--If you indeed know that, you would be wrong to hear me any farther. But if you are only in painful doubt about me, which makes you unwilling to run the risk of wasting your time, I will tell you beforehand what I really do think about this same liberty of action, namely, that whenever we can make a perfectly equitable law about any matter, or even a law securing, on the whole, more just conduct than unjust, we ought to make that law; and that there will yet, on these conditions, always remain a number of matters respecting which legalism and formalism are impossible; enough, and more than enough, to exercise all human powers of individual judgment, and afford all kinds of scope to individual character. I think this; but of course it can only be proved by separate examination of the possibilities of formal restraint in each given field of action; and these two lectures are nothing more than a sketch of such a detailed examination in one field, namely, that of art. You will find, however, one or two other remarks on such possibilities in the next note.

*　　　*　　　*　　　*　　　*

Note 2nd, p. 21.--"*Right to public support.*"

127. It did not appear to me desirable, in the course of the spoken lecture, to enter into details or offer suggestions on the questions of the regulation of labour and distribution of relief, as it would have been impossible to do so without touching on many disputed or disputable points, not easily handled before a general audience. But I must now supply what is wanting to make my general statement clear.

I believe, in the first place, that no Christian nation has any business to see one of its members in distress without helping him, though, perhaps, at the same time punishing him: help, of course--in nine cases out of ten--meaning guidance, much more than gift, and, therefore, interference with liberty. When a peasant mother sees one of her careless children fall into a ditch, her first proceeding is to pull him out; her second, to box his ears; her third, ordinarily, to lead him carefully a little way by the hand, or send him home for the rest of the day. The child usually cries, and very often would clearly prefer remaining in the ditch; and if he understood any of the terms of politics, would certainly express resentment at the interference with his individual liberty: but the mother has done her duty. Whereas the usual call of the mother nation to any of her children, under such circumstances, has lately been nothing more than the foxhunter's,--"Stay still there; I shall clear you." And if we always *could* clear them, their requests to be left in muddy independence might be sometimes allowed by kind people, or their cries for help disdained by unkind ones. But we can't clear them. The whole nation is, in fact, bound together, as men are by ropes on a glacier--if one falls, the rest must either lift him or drag him along with them[16] as dead weight, not without much increase of danger to themselves. And the law of right being manifestly in this--as, whether manifestly or not, it is always, the law of prudence--the only question is, how this wholesome help and interference are to be administered.

[Note 16: It is very curious to watch the efforts of two shop-keepers to ruin each other, neither having the least idea that his ruined neighbour must eventually be supported at his own expense, with an increase of poor rates; and that the contest between them is not in reality which shall get everything for himself, but which shall first take upon himself and his customers the gratuitous maintenance of the other's family.]

128. The first interference should be in education. In order that men may be able to support themselves when they are grown, their strength must be properly developed while they are young; and the State should always see to this--not allowing their health to be broken by too early labour, nor their powers to be wasted for want of knowledge. Some questions connected with this matter are noticed farther on under the head "trial schools": one point I must notice here, that I believe all youths, of whatever rank, ought to learn some manual trade thoroughly; for it is quite wonderful how much a man's views of life are cleared by the attainment of the capacity of doing any one thing well with his hands and arms. For a long time, what right life there was in the upper classes of Europe depended in no small degree on the necessity which each man was under of being able to fence; at this day, the most useful things which boys learn at public schools are, I believe, riding, rowing, and cricketing. But it would be far better that members of Parliament should be able to plough straight, and make a horseshoe, than only to feather oars neatly or point their toes prettily in stirrups. Then, in literary and scientific teaching, the great point of economy is to give the discipline of it through knowledge which will immediately bear on practical life. Our literary work has long been economically useless to us because too much concerned with dead languages; and our scientific

work will yet, for some time, be a good deal lost, because scientific men are too fond or too vain of their systems, and waste the student's time in endeavouring to give him large views, and make him perceive interesting connections of facts; when there is not one student, no, nor one man, in a thousand, who can feel the beauty of a system, or even take it clearly into his head; but nearly all men can understand, and most will be interested in, the facts which bear on daily life. Botanists have discovered some wonderful connection between nettles and figs, which a cowboy who will never see a ripe fig in his life need not be at all troubled about; but it will be interesting to him to know what effect nettles have on hay, and what taste they will give to porridge; and it will give him nearly a new life if he can be got but once, in a spring time, to look well at the beautiful circlet of white nettle blossom, and work out with his schoolmaster the curves of its petals, and the way it is set on its central mast. So, the principle of chemical equivalents, beautiful as it is, matters far less to a peasant boy, and even to most sons of gentlemen, than their knowing how to find whether the water is wholesome in the back-kitchen cistern, or whether the seven-acre field wants sand or chalk.

129. Having, then, directed the studies of our youth so as to make them practically serviceable men at the time of their entrance into life, that entrance should always be ready for them in cases where their private circumstances present no opening. There ought to be government establishments for every trade, in which all youths who desired it should be received as apprentices on their leaving school; and men thrown out of work received at all times. At these government manufactories the discipline should be strict, and the wages steady, not varying at all in proportion to the demand for the article, but only in proportion to the price of food; the commodities produced being laid up in store to meet sudden demands, and sudden fluctuations in prices prevented:--that gradual and necessary fluctuation only being allowed which is properly consequent on larger or more limited supply of raw material and other natural causes. When there was a visible tendency to produce a glut of any commodity, that tendency should be checked by directing the youth at the government schools into other trades; and the yearly surplus of commodities should be the principal means of government provisions for the poor. That provision should be large, and not disgraceful to them. At present there are very strange notions in the public mind respecting the receiving of alms: most people are will-

ing to take them in the form of a pension from government, but unwilling to take them in the form of a pension from their parishes. There may be some reason for this singular prejudice, in the fact of the government pension being usually given as a definite acknowledgment of some service done to the country;--but the parish pension is, or ought to be, given precisely on the same terms. A labourer serves his country with his spade, just as a man in the middle ranks of life serves it with his sword, pen, or lancet: if the service is less, and therefore the wages during health less, then the reward, when health is broken, may be less, but not, therefore, less honourable; and it ought to be quite as natural and straight-forward a matter for a labourer to take his pension from his parish, because he has deserved well of his parish, as for a man in higher rank to take his pension from his country, because he has deserved well of his country.

130. If there be any disgrace in coming to the parish, because it may imply improvidence in early life, much more is there disgrace in coming to the government: since improvidence is far less justifiable in a highly educated than in an imperfectly educated man; and far less justifiable in a high rank, where extravagance must have been luxury, than in a low rank, where it may only have been comfort. So that the real fact of the matter is, that people will take alms delightedly, consisting of a carriage and footmen, because those do not look like alms to the people in the street; but they will not take alms consisting only of bread and water and coals, because everybody would understand what those meant. Mind, I do not want any one to refuse the carriage who ought to have it; but neither do I want them to refuse the coals. I should indeed be sorry if any change in our views on these subjects involved the least lessening of self-dependence in the English mind: but the common shrinking of men from the acceptance of public charity is not self-dependence, but mere base and selfish pride. It is not that they are unwilling to live at their neighbours' expense, but that they are unwilling to confess they do: it is not dependence they wish to avoid, but gratitude. They will take places in which they know there is nothing to be done--they will borrow money they know they cannot repay--they will carry on a losing business with other people's capital--they will cheat the public in their shops, or sponge on their friends at their houses; but to say plainly they are poor men, who need the nation's help and go into an almshouse,--this they loftily repudiate, and virtuously prefer being thieves to being paupers.

131. I trust that these deceptive efforts of dishonest men to appear independent, and the agonizing efforts of unfortunate men to remain independent, may both be in some degree checked by a better administration and understanding of laws respecting the poor. But the ordinances for relief and the ordinances for labour must go together; otherwise distress caused by misfortune will always be confounded, as it is now, with distress caused by idleness, unthrift, and fraud. It is only when the State watches and guides the middle life of men, that it can, without disgrace to them, protect their old age, acknowledging in that protection that they have done their duty, or at least some portion of their duty, in better days.

I know well how strange, fanciful, or impracticable these suggestions will appear to most of the business men of this day; men who conceive the proper state of the world to be simply that of a vast and disorganized mob, scrambling each for what he can get, trampling down its children and old men in the mire, and doing what work it finds *must* be done with any irregular squad of labourers it can bribe or inveigle together, and afterwards scatter to starvation. A great deal may, indeed, be done in this way by a nation strong-elbowed and strong-hearted as we are--not easily frightened by pushing, nor discouraged by falls. But it is still not the right way of doing things, for people who call themselves Christians. Every so named soul of man claims from every other such soul, protection and education in childhood,--help or punishment in middle life,--reward or relief, if needed, in old age; all of these should be completely and unstintingly given; and they can only be given by the organization of such a system as I have described.

*   *   *   *   *

Note 3rd, p. 27.--"*Trial Schools.*"

132. It may be seriously questioned by the reader how much of painting talent we really lose on our present system,[17] and how much we should gain by the proposed trial schools. For it might be thought that, as matters stand at present, we have more painters than we ought to have, having so many bad ones, and that all youths who had true painters' genius forced their way out of obscurity.

[Note 17: It will be observed that, in the lecture, it is *assumed* that works of art are national treasures; and that it is desirable to withdraw all the hands capable of painting or carving from other employments, in order that they may produce this kind of wealth. I do not, in assuming this, mean that works of art add to the monetary resources of a nation, or form part of its wealth, in the vulgar sense. The result of the sale of a picture in the country itself is merely that a certain sum of money is transferred from the hands of B, the purchaser, to those of A, the producer; the sum ultimately to be distributed remaining the same, only A ultimately spending it instead of B, while the labour of A has been in the meantime withdrawn from productive channels; he has painted a picture which nobody can live upon, or live in, when he might have grown corn or built houses: when the sale therefore is effected in the country itself, it does not add to, but diminishes, the monetary resources of the country, except only so far as it may appear probable, on other grounds, that A is likely to spend the sum he receives for his picture more rationally and usefully than B would have spent it. If, indeed, the picture, or other work of art, be sold in foreign countries, either the money or the useful products of the foreign country being imported in exchange for it, such sale adds to the monetary resources of the selling, and diminishes those of the purchasing nation. But sound political economy, strange as it may at first appear to say so, has nothing whatever to do with separations between national interests. Political economy means the management of the affairs of **citizens**; and it either regards exclusively the administration of the affairs of one nation, or the administration of the affairs of the world considered as one nation. So when a transaction between individuals which enriches A impoverishes B in precisely the same degree, the sound economist considers it an unproductive transaction between the individuals; and if a trade between two nations which enriches one, impoverishes the other in the same degree, the sound economist considers it an unproductive trade between the nations. It is not a general question of political economy, but only a particular question of local expediency, whether an article, in itself valueless, may bear a value of exchange in transactions with some other nation. The economist considers only the actual value of the thing done or produced; and if he sees a quantity of labour spent, for instance, by the Swiss, in producing woodwork for sale to the English, he at once sets the commercial impoverishment of the English purchaser against the commercial enrichment of the Swiss seller; and considers the whole transaction productive only as far as the woodwork itself is a real addition to the wealth of the world. For the arrangement of the laws of a nation so as to procure the greatest advantages to itself, and leave the smallest advantages to other nations, is not a part of the science of political economy, but merely a broad application of the science of fraud. Considered thus in the abstract, pictures are not an ***addition*** to the monetary wealth of the world, except in the amount of pleasure or instruction to be got out of them day by day: but there is a certain protective effect on wealth exercised by works of high art which must always be included in the estimate of their value. Generally speaking, persons who decorate their houses with pictures will not spend so much money in papers, carpets, curtains, or other expensive and perishable luxuries as they would otherwise. Works of good art, like books, exercise a conservative effect on the rooms they are kept in; and the wall of the library or picture gallery remains undisturbed, when those of other rooms are repapered or re-panelled. Of course this effect is still more definite when the picture is on the walls themselves, either on canvas stretched into fixed shapes on their panels, or in fresco; involving, of course, the preservation of the building from all unnecessary and capricious alteration. And, generally speaking, the occupation of a large number of hands in painting or sculpture in any nation may be considered as tending to check the disposition to indulge in perishable luxury. I do not, however, in my assumption that works of art are treasures, take much into consideration this collateral monetary result. I consider them treasures, merely as permanent means of pleasure and instruction; and having at other times tried to show the several ways in which they can please and teach, assume here that they are thus useful, and that it is desirable to make as many painters as we can.]

This is not so. It is difficult to analyse the characters of mind which cause youths to mistake their vocation, and to endeavour to become artists, when they have no true artist's gift. But the fact is, that multitudes of young men do this, and that by far the greater number of living artists are men who have mistaken their vocation. The peculiar circumstances of modern life, which exhibit art in almost every form to the sight of the youths in our great cities, have a natural tendency to fill their imaginations with borrowed ideas, and their minds with imperfect science; the mere dislike of mechanical employments, either felt to be irksome, or believed to be degrading, urges numbers of young men to become painters, in the same temper in which they would enlist or go to sea; others, the sons of engravers or artists, taught the business of the art by their parents, and having no gift for it themselves, follow it as the means of livelihood, in an ignoble patience; or, if ambitious, seek to attract regard, or distance rivalry, by fantastic, meretricious, or unprecedented applications of their mechanical skill; while finally, many men, earnest in feeling, and conscientious in principle, mistake their desire to be useful for a love of art, and their quickness of emotion for its capacity, and pass their lives in painting moral and instructive pictures, which might almost justify us in thinking nobody could be a painter but a rogue. On the other hand, I believe that much of the best artistical intellect is daily lost in other avocations. Generally, the temper which would make an admirable artist is humble and observant, capable of taking much interest in little things, and of entertaining itself pleasantly in the dullest circumstances. Suppose, added to these characters, a steady conscientiousness which seeks to do its duty wherever it may be placed, and the power, denied to few artistical minds, of ingenious invention in almost any practical department of human skill, and it can hardly be doubted that the very humility and conscientiousness which would have perfected the painter, have in many instances prevented his becoming one; and that in the quiet life of our steady craftsmen--sagacious manufacturers, and uncomplaining clerks--there may frequently be concealed more genius than ever is raised to the direction of our public works, or to be the mark of our public praises.

133. It is indeed probable, that intense disposition for art will conquer the most formidable obstacles, if the surrounding circumstances are such as at all to present the idea of such conquest to the mind; but we have no ground for concluding that Giotto would ever have been more than a shepherd, if Cimabue had not by chance found him drawing; or that among the shepherds of the Apennines there were no other Giottos, undiscovered by Cimabue. We are too much in the habit of considering happy accidents as what are called 'special Providences'; and thinking that when any great work needs to be done, the man who is to do it will certainly be pointed out by Providence, be he shepherd or seaboy; and prepared for his work by all kinds of minor providences, in the best possible way. Whereas all the analogies of God's operations in other matters prove the contrary of this; we find that "of thousand seeds, He often brings but one to bear," often not one; and the one seed which He appoints to bear is allowed to bear crude or perfect fruit according to the dealings of the husbandman with it. And there cannot be a doubt in the mind of any person accustomed to take broad and logical views of the world's history, that its events are ruled by Providence in precisely the same manner as its harvests; that the seeds of good and evil are broadcast among men, just as the seeds of thistles

and fruits are; and that according to the force of our industry, and wisdom of our husbandry, the ground will bring forth to us figs or thistles. So that when it seems needed that a certain work should be done for the world, and no man is there to do it, we have no right to say that God did not wish it to be done; and therefore sent no men able to do it. The probability (if I wrote my own convictions, I should say certainty) is, that He sent many men, hundreds of men, able to do it; and that we have rejected them, or crushed them; by our previous folly of conduct or of institution, we have rendered it impossible to distinguish, or impossible to reach them; and when the need for them comes, and we suffer for the want of them, it is not that God refuses to send us deliverers, and specially appoints all our consequent sufferings; but that He has sent, and we have refused, the deliverers; and the pain is then wrought out by His eternal law, as surely as famine is wrought out by eternal law for a nation which will neither plough nor sow. No less are we in error in supposing, as we so frequently do, that if a man be found, he is sure to be in all respects fitted for the work to be done, as the key is to the lock: and that every accident which happened in the forging him, only adapted him more truly to the wards. It is pitiful to hear historians beguiling themselves and their readers, by tracing in the early history of great men the minor circumstances which fitted them for the work they did, without ever taking notice of the other circumstances which as assuredly unfitted them for it; so concluding that miraculous interposition prepared them in all points for everything, and that they did all that could have been desired or hoped for from them; whereas the certainty of the matter is that, throughout their lives, they were thwarted and corrupted by some things as certainly as they were helped and disciplined by others; and that, in the kindliest and most reverent view which can justly be taken of them, they were but poor mistaken creatures, struggling with a world more profoundly mistaken than they;--assuredly sinned against or sinning in thousands of ways, and bringing out at last a maimed result--not what they might or ought to have done, but all that could be done against the world's resistance, and in spite of their own sorrowful falsehood to themselves.

134. And this being so, it is the practical duty of a wise nation, first to withdraw, as far as may be, its youth from destructive influences;--then to try its material as far as possible, and to lose the use of none that is good. I do not mean by "withdrawing from destructive influences" the keeping of youths out of trials; but the keeping

them out of the way of things purely and absolutely mischievous. I do not mean that we should shade our green corn in all heat, and shelter it in all frost, but only that we should dyke out the inundation from it, and drive the fowls away from it. Let your youth labour and suffer; but do not let it starve, nor steal, nor blaspheme.

135. It is not, of course, in my power here to enter into details of schemes of education; and it will be long before the results of experiments now in progress will give data for the solution of the most difficult questions connected with the subject, of which the principal one is the mode in which the chance of advancement in life is to be extended to all, and yet made compatible with contentment in the pursuit of lower avocations by those whose abilities do not qualify them for the higher. But the general principle of trial schools lies at the root of the matter--of schools, that is to say, in which the knowledge offered and discipline enforced shall be all a part of a great assay of the human soul, and in which the one shall be increased, the other directed, as the tried heart and brain will best bear, and no otherwise. One thing, however, I must say, that in this trial I believe all emulation to be a false motive, and all giving of prizes a false means. All that you can depend upon in a boy, as significative of true power, likely to issue in good fruit, is his will to work for the work's sake, not his desire to surpass his school-fellows; and the aim of the teaching you give him ought to be, to prove to him and strengthen in him his own separate gift, not to puff him into swollen rivalry with those who are everlastingly greater than he: still less ought you to hang favours and ribands about the neck of the creature who is the greatest, to make the rest envy him. Try to make them love him and follow him, not struggle with him.

136. There must, of course, be examination to ascertain and attest both progress and relative capacity; but our aim should be to make the students rather look upon it as a means of ascertaining their own true positions and powers in the world, than as an arena in which to carry away a present victory. I have not, perhaps, in the course of the lecture, insisted enough on the nature of relative capacity and individual character, as the roots of all real *value* in Art. We are too much in the habit, in these days, of acting as if Art worth a price in the market were a commodity which people could be generally taught to produce, and as if the ***education*** of the artist, not his ***capacity***, gave the sterling value to his work. No impression can possibly be more absurd or false. Whatever people can teach each other to do, they will

estimate, and ought to estimate, only as common industry; nothing will ever fetch a high price but precisely that which cannot be taught, and which nobody can do but the man from whom it is purchased. No state of society, nor stage of knowledge, ever does away with the natural pre-eminence of one man over another; and it is that pre-eminence, and that only, which will give work high value in the market, or which ought to do so. It is a bad sign of the judgment, and bad omen for the progress, of a nation, if it supposes itself to possess many artists of equal merit. Noble art is nothing less than the expression of a great soul; and great souls are not common things. If ever we confound their work with that of others, it is not through liberality, but through blindness.

*　　*　　*　　*　　*

Note 4th, p. 28.--"*Public favour.*"

137. There is great difficulty in making any short or general statement of the difference between great and ignoble minds in their behaviour to the 'public.' It is by no means ***universally*** the case that a mean mind, as stated in the text, will bend itself to what you ask of it: on the contrary, there is one kind of mind, the meanest of all, which perpetually complains of the public, and contemplates and proclaims itself as a 'genius,' refuses all wholesome discipline or humble office, and ends in miserable and revengeful ruin; also, the greatest minds are marked by nothing more distinctly than an inconceivable humility, and acceptance of work or instruction in any form, and from any quarter. They will learn from everybody, and do anything that anybody asks of them, so long as it involves only toil, or what other men would think degradation. But the point of quarrel, nevertheless, assuredly rises some day between the public and them, respecting some matter, not of humiliation, but of Fact. Your great man always at last comes to see something the public don't see. This something he will assuredly persist in asserting, whether with tongue or pencil, to be as *he* sees it, not as *they* see it; and all the world in a heap on the other side, will not get him to say otherwise. Then, if the world objects to the saying, he may happen to get stoned or burnt for it, but that does not in the least matter to him; if the world has no particular objection to the saying, he may get leave to mutter it to himself till he dies, and be merely taken for an idiot; that also does not matter to him--mutter it he will, according to what he perceives to be fact, and not at all according to the roaring of the walls of Red Sea on the right hand or left of him.

Hence the quarrel, sure at some time or other to be started between the public and him; while your mean man, though he will spit and scratch spiritedly at the public, while it does not attend to him, will bow to it for its clap in any direction, and say anything when he has got its ear, which he thinks will bring him another clap; and thus, as stated in the text, he and it go on smoothly together.

There are, however, times when the obstinacy of the mean man looks very like the obstinacy of the great one; but if you look closely into the matter, you will always see that the obstinacy of the first is in the pronunciation of "I;" and of the second, in the pronunciation of "It."

*   *   *   *   *

Note 5th, p. 56.--"*Invention of new wants.*"

138. It would have been impossible for political economists long to have endured the error spoken of in the text,[18] had they not been confused by an idea, in part well founded, that the energies and refinements, as well as the riches of civilised life, arose from imaginary wants. It is quite true, that the savage who knows no needs but those of food, shelter, and sleep, and after he has snared his venison and patched the rents of his hut, passes the rest of his time in animal repose, is in a lower state than the man who labours incessantly that he may procure for himself the luxuries of civilisation; and true also, that the difference between one and another nation in progressive power depends in great part on vain desires; but these idle motives are merely to be considered as giving exercise to the national body and mind; they are not sources of wealth, except so far as they give the habits of industry and acquisitiveness. If a boy is clumsy and lazy, we shall do good if we can persuade him to carve cherry-stones and fly kites; and this use of his fingers and limbs may eventually be the cause of his becoming a wealthy and happy man; but we must not therefore argue that cherry-stones are valuable property, or that kite-flying is a profitable mode of passing time. In like manner, a nation always wastes its time and labour **directly**, when it invents a new want of a frivolous kind, and yet the invention of such a want may be the sign of a healthy activity, and the labour undergone to satisfy the new want may lead, **indirectly**, to useful discoveries or to noble arts; so that a nation is not to be discouraged in its fancies when it is either too weak or foolish to be moved to exertion by anything but fancies, or has attended to its serious business first. If a nation will not forge iron, but likes distilling lavender, by all

means give it lavender to distil; only do not let its economists suppose that lavender is as profitable to it as oats, or that it helps poor people to live, any more than the schoolboy's kite provides him his dinner. Luxuries, whether national or personal, must be paid for by labour withdrawn from useful things; and no nation has a right to indulge in them until all its poor are comfortably housed and fed.

[Note 18: I have given the political economist too much credit in saying this. Actually, while these sheets are passing through the press, the blunt, broad, unmitigated fallacy is enunciated, formally and precisely, by the common councilmen of New York, in their report on the present commercial crisis. Here is their collective opinion, published in the *Times* of November 23rd, 1857:--"Another erroneous idea is that luxurious living, extravagant dressing, splendid turn-outs and fine houses, are the cause of distress to a nation. No more erroneous impression could exist. Every extravagance that the man of 100,000 or 1,000,000 dollars indulges in adds to the means, the support, the wealth of ten or a hundred who had little or nothing else but their labour, their intellect, or their taste. If a man of 1,000,000 dollars spends principal and interest in ten years, and finds himself beggared at the end of that time, he has actually made a hundred who have catered to his extravagance, employers or employed, so much richer by the division of his wealth. He may be ruined, but the nation is better off and richer, for one hundred minds and hands, with 10,000 dollars apiece, are far more productive than one with the whole."

Yes, gentlemen of the common council; but what has been doing in the time of the transfer? The spending of the fortune has taken a certain number of years (suppose ten), and during that time 1,000,000 dollars' worth of work has been done by the people, who have been paid that sum for it. Where is the product of that work? By your own statements, wholly consumed; for the man for whom it has been done is now a beggar. You have given therefore, as a nation, 1,000,000 dollars' worth of work, and ten years of time, and you have produced, as ultimate result, one beggar. Excellent economy, gentlemen! and sure to conduce, in due sequence, to the production of *more* than one beggar. Perhaps the matter may be made clearer to you, however, by a more familiar instance. If a schoolboy goes out in the morning with five shillings in his pocket, and comes home penniless, having spent his all in tarts, principal and interest are gone, and fruiterer and baker are enriched. So far so good. But suppose the schoolboy, instead, has bought a book and a knife; principal and interest are gone, and book-seller and cutler are enriched. But the schoolboy is en-riched also, and may help his school-fellows next day with knife and book, instead of lying in bed and incurring a debt to the doctor.]

139. The enervating influence of luxury, and its tendencies to increase vice, are points which I keep entirely out of consideration in the present essay; but, so far as they bear on any question discussed, they merely furnish additional evidence on the side which I have taken. Thus, in the present case, I assume that the luxuries of civilized life are in possession harmless, and in acquirement serviceable as a motive for exertion; and even on those favourable terms, we arrive at the conclusion that the nation ought not to indulge in them except under severe limitations. Much less ought it to indulge in them if the temptation consequent on their possession, or fatality incident to their manufacture, more than counter-balances the good done by the effort to obtain them.

*   *   *   *   *

Note 6th, p. 74.--"*Economy of literature.*"

140. I have been much impressed lately by one of the results of the quantity of our books; namely, the stern impossibility of getting anything understood, that required patience to understand. I observe always, in the case of my own writings, that if ever I state anything which has cost me any trouble to ascertain, and which, therefore, will probably require a minute or two of reflection from the reader be-fore it can be accepted,--that statement will not only be misunderstood, but in all probability taken to mean something very nearly the reverse of what it does mean. Now, whatever faults there may be in my modes of expression, I know that the words I use will always be found, by Johnson's dictionary, to bear, first of all, the sense I use them in; and that the sentences, whether awkwardly turned or not, will, by the ordinary rules of grammar, bear no other interpretation than that I mean them to bear; so that the misunderstanding of them must result, ultimately, from the mere fact that their matter sometimes requires a little patience. And I see the same kind of misinterpretation put on the words of other writers, whenever they require the same kind of thought.

141. I was at first a little despondent about this; but, on the whole, I believe it will have a good effect upon our literature for some time to come; and then, per-haps, the public may recover its patience again. For certainly it is excellent disci-

pline for an author to feel that he must say all he has to say in the fewest possible words, or his reader is sure to skip them; and in the plainest possible words, or his reader will certainly misunderstand them. Generally, also, a downright fact may be told in a plain way; and we want downright facts at present more than anything else. And though I often hear moral people complaining of the bad effects of want of thought, for my part, it seems to me that one of the worst diseases to which the human creature is liable is its disease of thinking. If it would only just *look*[19] at a thing instead of thinking what it must be like, or *do* a thing instead of thinking it cannot be done, we should all get on far better.

[Note 19: There can be no question, however, of the mischievous tendency of the hurry of the present day, in the way people undertake this very *looking*. I gave three years' close and incessant labour to the examination of the chronology of the architecture of Venice; two long winters being wholly spent in the drawing of details on the spot; and yet I see constantly that architects who pass three or four days in a gondola going up and down the Grand Canal, think that their first impressions are just as likely to be true as my patiently wrought conclusions. Mr. Street, for instance, glances hastily at the facade of the Ducal Palace--so hastily that he does not even see what its pattern is, and misses the alternation of red and black in the centres of its squares--and yet he instantly ventures on an opinion on the chronology of its capitals, which is one of the most complicated and difficult subjects in the whole range of Gothic archaeology. It may, nevertheless, be ascertained with very fair probability of correctness by any person who will give a month's hard work to it, but it can be ascertained no otherwise.]

    *   *   *   *   *

Note 7th, p. 147.--"*Pilots of the State.*"

142. While, however, undoubtedly, these responsibilities attach to every person possessed of wealth, it is necessary both to avoid any stringency of statement respecting the benevolent modes of spending money, and to admit and approve so much liberty of spending it for selfish pleasures as may distinctly make wealth a personal *reward* for toil, and secure in the minds of all men the right of property. For although, without doubt, the purest pleasures it can procure are not selfish, it is only as a means of personal gratification that it will be desired by a large majority of workers; and it would be no less false ethics than false policy to check their energy

by any forms of public opinion which bore hardly against the wanton expenditure of honestly got wealth. It would be hard if a man who has passed the greater part of his life at the desk or counter could not at last innocently gratify a caprice; and all the best and most sacred ends of almsgiving would be at once disappointed, if the idea of a moral claim took the place of affectionate gratitude in the mind of the receiver.

143. Some distinction is made by us naturally in this respect between earned and inherited wealth; that which is inherited appearing to involve the most definite responsibilities, especially when consisting in revenues derived from the soil. The form of taxation which constitutes rental of lands places annually a certain portion of the national wealth in the hands of the nobles, or other proprietors of the soil, under conditions peculiarly calculated to induce them to give their best care to its efficient administration. The want of instruction in even the simplest principles of commerce and economy, which hitherto has disgraced our schools and universities, has indeed been the cause of ruin or total inutility of life to multitudes of our men of estate; but this deficiency in our public education cannot exist much longer, and it appears to be highly advantageous for the State that a certain number of persons distinguished by race should be permitted to set examples of wise expenditure, whether in the advancement of science, or in patronage of art and literature; only they must see to it that they take their right standing more firmly than they have done hitherto, for the position of a rich man in relation to those around him is, in our present real life, and is also contemplated generally by political economists as being, precisely the reverse of what it ought to be. A rich man ought to be continually examining how he may spend his money for the advantage of others: at present, others are continually plotting how they may beguile him into spending it apparently for his own. The aspect which he presents to the eyes of the world is generally that of a person holding a bag of money with a staunch grasp, and resolved to part with none of it unless he is forced, and all the people about him are plotting how they may force him: that is to say, how they may persuade him that he wants this thing or that; or how they may produce things that he will covet and buy. One man tries to persuade him that he wants perfumes; another that he wants jewellery; another that he wants sugarplums; another that he wants roses at Christmas. Anybody who can invent a new want for him is supposed to be a benefactor

to society: and thus the energies of the poorer people about him are continually directed to the production of covetable, instead of serviceable, things; and the rich man has the general aspect of a fool, plotted against by the world. Whereas the real aspect which he ought to have is that of a person wiser than others, entrusted with the management of a larger quantity of capital, which he administers for the profit of all, directing each man to the labour which is most healthy for him, and most serviceable for the community.

*   *   *   *   *

Note 8th, p. 148.--"*Silk and purple.*"

144. In various places throughout these lectures I have had to allude to the distinction between productive and unproductive labour, and between true and false wealth. I shall here endeavour, as clearly as I can, to explain the distinction I mean.

Property may be divided generally into two kinds; that which produces life, and that which produces the objects of life. That which produces or maintains life consists of food, in so far as it is nourishing; of furniture and clothing, in so far as they are protective or cherishing; of fuel; and of all land, instruments, or materials necessary to produce food, houses, clothes, and fuel. It is specially and rightly called useful property.

The property which produces the objects of life consists of all that gives pleasure or suggests and preserves thought: of food, furniture, and land, in so far as they are pleasing to the appetite or the eye; of luxurious dress, and all other kinds of luxuries; of books, pictures, and architecture. But the modes of connection of certain minor forms of property with human labour render it desirable to arrange them under more than these two heads. Property may therefore be conveniently considered as of five kinds.

145. (1) Property necessary to life, but not producible by labour, and therefore belonging of right, in a due measure, to every human being as soon as he is born, and morally inalienable. As for instance, his proper share of the atmosphere, without which he cannot breathe, and of water, which he needs to quench his thirst. As much land as he needs to feed from is also inalienable; but in well-regulated communities this quantity of land may often be represented by other possessions, or its need supplied by wages and privileges.

(2) Property necessary to life, but only producible by labour, and of which the possession is morally connected with labour, so that no person capable of doing the work necessary for its production has a right to it until he has done that work;--"he that will not work, neither should he eat." It consists of simple food, clothing, and habitation, with their seeds and materials, or instruments and machinery, and animals used for necessary draught or locomotion, etc. It is to be observed of this kind of property, that its increase cannot usually be carried beyond a certain point, because it depends not on labour only, but on things of which the supply is limited by nature. The possible accumulation of corn depends on the quantity of corn-growing land possessed or commercially accessible; and that of steel, similarly on the accessible quantity of coal and iron-stone. It follows from this natural limitation of supply that the accumulation of property of this kind in large masses at one point, or in one person's hands, commonly involves, more or less, the scarcity of it at another point and in other persons' hands; so that the accidents or energies which may enable one man to procure a great deal of it, may, and in all likelihood will, partially prevent other men procuring a sufficiency of it, however willing they may be to work for it; therefore, the modes of its accumulation and distribution need to be in some degree regulated by law and by national treaties, in order to secure justice to all men.

Another point requiring notice respecting this sort of property is, that no work can be wasted in producing it, provided only the kind of it produced be preservable and distributable, since for every grain of such commodities we produce we are rendering so much more life possible on earth.[20] But though we are sure, thus, that we are employing people well, we cannot be sure we might not have employed them **better**; for it is possible to direct labour to the production of life, until little or none is left for that of the objects of life, and thus to increase population at the expense of civilization, learning, and morality: on the other hand, it is just as possible--and the error is one to which the world is, on the whole, more liable--to direct labour to the objects of life till too little is left for life, and thus to increase luxury or learning at the expense of population. Right political economy holds its aim poised justly between the two extremes, desiring neither to crowd its dominions with a race of savages, nor to found courts and colleges in the midst of a desert.

[Note 20: This point has sometimes been disputed; for instance, opening Mill's 'Political Economy' the other day, I chanced on a passage in which he says that a man who makes a coat, if the person who wears the coat does nothing useful while he wears it, has done no more good to society than the man who has only raised a pineapple. But this is a fallacy induced by endeavour after too much subtlety. None of us have a right to say that the life of a man is of no use to *him*, though it may be of no use to *us*; and the man who made the coat, and thereby prolonged another man's life, has done a gracious and useful work, whatever may come of the life so prolonged. We may say to the wearer of the coat, "You who are wearing coats, and doing nothing in them, are at present wasting your own life and other people's;" but we have no right to say that his existence, however wasted, is wasted *away*. It may be just dragging itself on, in its thin golden line, with nothing dependent upon it, to the point where it is to strengthen into good chain cable, and have thousands of other lives dependent on it. Meantime, the simple fact respecting the coat-maker is, that he has given so much life to the creature, the results of which he cannot calculate; they may be--in all probability will be--infinite results in some way. But the raiser of pines, who has only given a pleasant taste in the mouth to some one, may see with tolerable clearness to the end of the taste in the mouth, and of all conceivable results therefrom.]

146. (3) The third kind of property is that which conduces to bodily pleasures and conveniences, without directly tending to sustain life; perhaps sometimes indirectly tending to destroy it. All dainty (as distinguished from nourishing) food, and means of producing it; all scents not needed for health; substances valued only for their appearance and rarity (as gold and jewels); flowers of difficult culture; animals used for delight (as horses for racing), and such like, form property of this class; to which the term 'luxury,' or 'luxuries,' ought exclusively to belong.

Respecting which we have to note, first, that all such property is of doubtful advantage even to its possessor. Furniture tempting to indolence, sweet odours, and luscious food, are more or less injurious to health: while jewels, liveries, and other such common belongings of wealthy people, certainly convey no pleasure to their owners proportionate to their cost.

Farther, such property, for the most part, perishes in the using. Jewels form a great exception--but rich food, fine dresses, horses and carriages, are consumed by the owner's use. It ought much oftener to be brought to the notice of rich men what sums of interest of money they are paying towards the close of their lives, for luxuries consumed in the middle of them. It would be very interesting, for instance, to know the exact sum which the money spent in London for ices, at its desserts and balls, during the last twenty years, had it been saved and put out at compound interest, would at this moment have furnished for useful purposes.

Also, in most cases, the enjoyment of such property is wholly selfish, and limited to its possessor. Splendid dress and equipage, however, when so arranged as to produce real beauty of effect, may often be rather a generous than a selfish channel of expenditure. They will, however, necessarily in such cases involve some of the arts of design; and therefore take their place in a higher category than that of luxuries merely.

147. (4) The fourth kind of property is that which bestows intellectual or emotional pleasure, consisting of land set apart for purposes of delight more than for agriculture, of books, works of art, and objects of natural history.

It is, of course, impossible to fix an accurate limit between property of the last class and of this class, since things which are a mere luxury to one person are a means of intellectual occupation to another. Flowers in a London ball-room are a luxury; in a botanical garden, a delight of the intellect; and in their native fields, both; while the most noble works of art are continually made material of vulgar luxury or of criminal pride; but, when rightly used, property of this fourth class is the only kind which deserves the name of *real* property, it is the only kind which a man can truly be said to 'possess.' What a man eats, or drinks, or wears, so long as it is only what is needful for life, can no more be thought of as his possession than the air he breathes. The air is as needful to him as the food; but we do not talk of a man's wealth of air, and what food or clothing a man possesses more than he himself requires must be for others to use (and, to him, therefore, not a real property in itself, but only a means of obtaining some real property in exchange for it). Whereas the things that give intellectual or emotional enjoyment may be accumulated, and do not perish in using; but continually supply new pleasures and new powers of giving pleasures to others. And these, therefore, are the only things which can rightly be thought of as giving 'wealth' or 'well being.' Food conduces only to 'being,' but these to '*well* being.' And there is not any broader general distinction between lower and higher orders of men than rests on their possession of this real property. The human race may be properly divided by zoologists into "men who have gardens, libraries, or works of art; and those who have none;" and the former class will include all noble persons, except only a few who make the world their garden or museum; while the people who have not, or, which is the same thing, do not care for gardens or libraries, but care for nothing but money or luxuries, will include none but ignoble persons: only it is necessary to understand that I mean by the term 'garden' as much the Carthusian's plot of ground fifteen feet square between his monastery buttresses, as I do the grounds of Chatsworth or Kew; and I mean by the term 'art' as much the old sailor's print of the ***Arethusa*** bearing up to engage the ***Belle Poule***, as I do Raphael's "Disputa," and even rather more; for when abundant, beautiful possessions of this kind are almost always associated with vulgar luxury, and become then anything but indicative of noble character in their possessors. The ideal of human life is a union of Spartan simplicity of manners with Athenian sensibility and imagination; but in actual results, we are continually mistaking ignorance for simplicity, and sensuality for refinement.

148. (5) The fifth kind of property is representative property, consisting of documents or money, or rather documents only--for money itself is only a transferable document, current among societies of men, giving claim, at sight, to some definite benefit or advantage, most commonly to a certain share of real property existing in those societies. The money is only genuine when the property it gives claim to is real, or the advantages it gives claim to certain; otherwise, it is false money, and may be considered as much 'forged' when issued by a government, or a bank, as when by an individual. Thus, if a dozen of men, cast ashore on a desert island, pick up a number of stones, put a red spot on each stone, and pass a law that every stone marked with a red spot shall give claim to a peck of wheat;--so long as no wheat exists, or can exist, on the island, the stones are not money. But the moment as much wheat exists as shall render it possible for the society always to give a peck for every spotted stone, the spotted stones would become money, and might be exchanged by their possessors for whatever other commodities they chose, to the value of the peck of wheat which the stones represented. If more stones were issued than the quantity of wheat could answer the demand of, the value of the stone coinage would be depreciated, in proportion to its increase above the quantity needed to answer it.

149. Again, supposing a certain number of the men so cast ashore were set aside

by lot, or any other convention, to do the rougher labour necessary for the whole society, they themselves being maintained by the daily allotment of a certain quantity of food, clothing, etc. Then, if it were agreed that the stones spotted with red should be signs of a Government order for the labour of these men; and that any person presenting a spotted stone at the office of the labourers, should be entitled to a man's work for a week or a day, the red stones would be money; and might--probably would--immediately pass current in the island for as much food, or clothing, or iron, or any other article, as a man's work for the period secured by the stone was worth. But if the Government issued so many spotted stones that it was impossible for the body of men they employed to comply with the orders,--as, suppose, if they only employed twelve men, and issued eighteen spotted stones daily, ordering a day's work each,--then the six extra stones would be forged or false money; and the effect of this forgery would be the depreciation of the value of the whole coinage by one-third, that being the period of shortcoming which would, on the average, necessarily ensue in the execution of each order. Much occasional work may be done in a state or society, by help of an issue of false money (or false promises) by way of stimulants; and the fruit of this work, if it comes into the promiser's hands, may sometimes enable the false promises at last to be fulfilled: hence the frequent issue of false money by governments and banks, and the not unfrequent escapes from the natural and proper consequences of such false issues, so as to cause a confused conception in most people's minds of what money really is. I am not sure whether some quantity of such false issue may not really be permissible in a nation, accurately proportioned to the minimum average produce of the labour it excites; but all such procedures are more or less unsound; and the notion of unlimited issue of currency is simply one of the absurdest and most monstrous that ever came into disjointed human wits.

150. The use of objects of real or supposed value for currency, as gold, jewellery, etc., is barbarous; and it always expresses either the measure of the distrust in the society of its own government, or the proportion of distrustful or barbarous nations with whom it has to deal. A metal not easily corroded or imitated, it is a desirable medium of currency for the sake of cleanliness and convenience, but, were it possible to prevent forgery, the more worthless the metal itself, the better. The use of worthless media, unrestrained by the use of valuable media, has always hitherto

involved, and is therefore supposed to involve necessarily, unlimited, or at least improperly extended, issue; but we might as well suppose that a man must necessarily issue unlimited promises because his words cost nothing. Intercourse with foreign nations must, indeed, for ages yet to come, at the world's present rate of progress, be carried on by valuable currencies; but such transactions are nothing more than forms of barter. The gold used at present as a currency is not, in point of fact, currency at all, but the real property[21] which the currency gives claim to, stamped to measure its quantity, and mingling with the real currency occasionally by barter.

151. The evils necessarily resulting from the use of baseless currencies have been terribly illustrated while these sheets have been passing through the press; I have not had time to examine the various conditions of dishonest or absurd trading which have led to the late 'panic' in America and England; this only I know, that no merchant deserving the name ought to be more liable to 'panic' than a soldier should; for his name should never be on more paper than he can at any instant meet the call of, happen what will. I do not say this without feeling at the same time how difficult it is to mark, in existing commerce, the just limits between the spirit of enterprise and of speculation. Something of the same temper which makes the English soldier do always all that is possible, and attempt more than is possible, joins its influence with that of mere avarice in tempting the English merchant into risks which he cannot justify, and efforts which he cannot sustain; and the same passion for adventure which our travellers gratify every summer on perilous snow wreaths, and cloud-encompassed precipices, surrounds with a romantic fascination the glittering of a hollow investment, and gilds the clouds that curl round gulfs of ruin. Nay, a higher and a more serious feeling frequently mingles in the motley temptation; and men apply themselves to the task of growing rich, as to a labour of providential appointment, from which they cannot pause without culpability, nor retire without dishonour. Our large trading cities bear to me very nearly the aspect of monastic establishments in which the roar of the mill-wheel and the crane takes the place of other devotional music; and in which the worship of Mammon or Moloch is conducted with a tender reverence and an exact propriety; the merchant rising to his Mammon matins with the self-denial of an anchorite, and expiating the frivolities into which he may be beguiled in the course of the day by late attendance at Mammon vespers. But, with every allowance that can be made for these con-

scientious and romantic persons, the fact remains the same, that by far the greater number of the transactions which lead to these times of commercial embarrassment may be ranged simply under two great heads--gambling and stealing; and both of these in their most culpable form, namely, gambling with money which is not ours, and stealing from those who trust us. I have sometimes thought a day might come, when the nation would perceive that a well-educated man who steals a hundred thousand pounds, involving the entire means of subsistence of a hundred families, deserves, on the whole, as severe a punishment as an ill-educated man who steals a purse from a pocket, or a mug from a pantry.

[Note 21: Or rather, equivalent to such real property, because everybody has been accustomed to look upon it as valuable; and therefore everybody is willing to give labour or goods for it. But real property does ultimately consist only in things that nourish body or mind; gold would be useless to us if we could not get mutton or books for it. Ultimately all commercial mistakes and embarrassments result from people expecting to get goods without working for them, or wasting them after they have got them. A nation which labours, and takes care of the fruits of labour, would be rich and happy though there were no gold in the universe. A nation which is idle, and wastes the produce of what work it does, would be poor and miserable, though all its mountains were of gold, and had glens filled with diamond instead of glacier.]

152. But without hoping for this excess of clear-sightedness, we may at least labour for a system of greater honesty and kindness in the minor commerce of our daily life; since the great dishonesty of the great buyers and sellers is nothing more than the natural growth and outcome from the little dishonesty of the little buyers and sellers. Every person who tries to buy an article for less than its proper value, or who tries to sell it at more than its proper value--every consumer who keeps a tradesman waiting for his money, and every tradesman who bribes a consumer to extravagance by credit, is helping forward, according to his own measure of power, a system of baseless and dishonourable commerce, and forcing his country down into poverty and shame. And people of moderate means and average powers of mind would do far more real good by merely carrying out stern principles of justice and honesty in common matters of trade, than by the most ingenious schemes of extended philanthropy, or vociferous declarations of theological doctrine. There

are three weighty matters of the law--justice, mercy, and truth; and of these the Teacher puts truth last, because that cannot be known but by a course of acts of justice and love. But men put, in all their efforts, truth first, because they mean by it their own opinions; and thus, while the world has many people who would suffer martyrdom in the cause of what they call truth, it has few who will suffer even a little inconvenience, in that of justice and mercy.

SUPPLEMENTARY ADDITIONAL PAPERS.
EDUCATION IN ART.
ART SCHOOL NOTES.
SOCIAL POLICY.
EDUCATION IN ART.

(*Read for the author before the National Association for the Promotion of Social Science in the autumn of 1858; and printed in the Transactions of the Society for that year, pp. 311-16.*)

153. I will not attempt in this paper to enter into any general consideration of the possible influence of art on the masses of the people. The inquiry is one of great complexity, involved with that into the uses and dangers of luxury; nor have we as yet data enough to justify us in conjecturing how far the practice of art may be compatible with rude or mechanical employments. But the question, however difficult, lies in the same light as that of the uses of reading or writing; for drawing, so far as it is possible to the multitude, is mainly to be considered as a means of obtaining and communicating knowledge. He who can accurately represent the form of an object, and match its colour, has unquestionably a power of notation and description greater in most instances than that of words; and this science of notation ought to be simply regarded as that which is concerned with the record of form, just as arithmetic is concerned with the record of number. Of course abuses and dangers attend the acquirement of every power. We have all of us probably known persons who, without being able to read or write, discharged the important duties of life wisely and faithfully; as we have also without doubt known others able to read and write whose reading did little good to themselves and whose writing little good to any one else. But we do not therefore doubt the expediency of acquiring those arts, neither ought we to doubt the expediency of acquiring the art of drawing, if we

admit that it may indeed become practically useful.

154. Nor should we long hesitate in admitting this, it we were not in the habit of considering instruction in the arts chiefly as a means of promoting what we call "taste" or dilettanteism, and other habits of mind which in their more modern developments in Europe have certainly not been advantageous to nations, or indicative of worthiness in them. Nevertheless, true taste, or the instantaneous preference of the noble thing to the ignoble, is a necessary accompaniment of high worthiness in nations or men; only it is not to be acquired by seeking it as our chief object, since the first question, alike for man and for multitude, is not at all what they are to like, but what they are to do; and fortunately so, since true taste, so far as it depends on original instinct, is not equally communicable to all men; and, so far as it depends on extended comparison, is unattainable by men employed in narrow fields of life. We shall not succeed in making a peasant's opinion good evidence on the merits of the Elgin and Lycian marbles; nor is it necessary to dictate to him in his garden the preference of gillyflower or of rose; yet I believe we may make art a means of giving him helpful and happy pleasure, and of gaining for him serviceable knowledge.

155. Thus, in our simplest codes of school instruction, I hope some day to see local natural history assume a principal place, so that our peasant children may be taught the nature and uses of the herbs that grow in their meadows, and may take interest in observing and cherishing, rather than in hunting or killing, the harmless animals of their country. Supposing it determined that this local natural history should be taught, drawing ought to be used to fix the attention, and test, while it aided, the memory. "Draw such and such a flower in outline, with its bell towards you. Draw it with its side towards you. Paint the spots upon it. Draw a duck's head--her foot. Now a robin's--a thrush's--now the spots upon the thrush's breast." These are the kinds of tasks which it seems to me should be set to the young peasant student. Surely the occupation would no more be thought contemptible which was thus subservient to knowledge and to compassion; and perhaps we should find in process of time that the Italian connexion of art with *diletto*, or delight, was both consistent with, and even mainly consequent upon, a pure Greek connexion of art with *arete*, or virtue.

156. It may perhaps be thought that the power of representing in any sufficient manner natural objects such as those above instanced would be of too difficult at-

tainment to be aimed at in elementary instruction. But I have had practical proof that it is not so. From workmen who had little time to spare, and that only after they were jaded by the day's labour, I have obtained, in the course of three or four months from their first taking a pencil in hand, perfectly useful, and in many respects admirable, drawings of natural objects. It is, however, necessary, in order to secure this result, that the student's aim should be absolutely restricted to the representation of visible fact. All more varied or elevated practice must be deferred until the powers of true sight and just representation are acquired in simplicity; nor, in the case of children belonging to the lower classes, does it seem to me often advisable to aim at anything more. At all events, their drawing lessons should be made as recreative as possible. Undergoing due discipline of hard labour in other directions, such children should be painlessly initiated into employments calculated for the relief of toil. It is of little consequence that they should know the principles of art, but of much that their attention should be pleasurably excited. In our higher public schools, on the contrary, drawing should be taught rightly; that is to say, with due succession and security of preliminary steps,--it being here of little consequence whether the student attains great or little skill, but of much that he should perceive distinctly what degree of skill he has attained, reverence that which surpasses it, and know the principles of right in what he has been able to accomplish. It is impossible to make every boy an artist or a connoisseur, but quite possible to make him understand the meaning of art in its rudiments, and to make him modest enough to forbear expressing, in after life, judgments which he has not knowledge enough to render just.

157. There is, however, at present this great difficulty in the way of such systematic teaching--that the public do not believe the principles of art are determinable, and, in no wise, matters of opinion. They do not believe that good drawing is good, and bad drawing bad, whatever any number of persons may think or declare to the contrary--that there is a right or best way of laying colours to produce a given effect, just as there is a right or best way of dyeing cloth of a given colour, and that Titian and Veronese are not merely accidentally admirable but eternally right.

158. The public, of course, cannot be convinced of this unity and stability of principle until clear assertion of it is made to them by painters whom they respect; and the painters whom they respect are generally too modest, and sometimes too

proud, to make it. I believe the chief reason for their not having yet declared at least the fundamental laws of labour as connected with art-study is a kind of feeling on their part that "***cela va sans dire***." Every great painter knows so well the necessity of hard and systematized work, in order to attain even the lower degrees of skill, that he naturally supposes if people use no diligence in drawing, they do not care to acquire the power of it, and that the toil involved in wholesome study being greater than the mass of people have ever given, is also greater than they would ever be willing to give. Feeling, also, as any real painter feels, that his own excellence is a gift, no less than the reward of toil, perhaps slightly disliking to confess the labour it has cost him to perfect it, and wholly despairing of doing any good by the confession, he contemptuously leaves the drawing-master to do the best he can in his twelve lessons, and with courteous unkindness permits the young women of England to remain under the impression that they can learn to draw with less pains than they can learn to dance. I have had practical experience enough, however, to convince me that this treatment of the amateur student is unjust. Young girls will work with steadiest perseverance when once they understand the need of labour, and are convinced that drawing is a kind of language which may for ordinary purposes be learned as easily as French or German; this language, also, having its grammar and its pronunciation, to be conquered or acquired only by persistence in irksome exercise--an error in a form being as entirely and simply an error as a mistake in a tense, and an ill-drawn line as reprehensible as a vulgar accent.

159. And I attach great importance to the sound education of our younger females in art, thinking that in England the nursery and the drawing-room are perhaps the most influential of academies. We address ourselves in vain to the education of the artist while the demand for his work is uncertain or unintelligent; nor can art be considered as having any serious influence on a nation while gilded papers form the principal splendour of the reception room, and ill-wrought though costly trinkets the principal entertainment of the boudoir.

It is surely, therefore, to be regretted that the art-education of our Government schools is addressed so definitely to the guidance of the artizan, and is therefore so little acknowledged hitherto by the general public, especially by its upper classes. I have not acquaintance enough with the practical working of that system to venture any expression of opinion respecting its general expediency; but it is my conviction that, so far as references are involved in it to the designing of patterns capable of being produced by machinery, such references must materially diminish its utility considered as a general system of instruction.

160. We are still, therefore, driven to the same point,--the need of an authoritative recommendation of some method of study to the public; a method determined upon by the concurrence of some of our best painters, and avowedly sanctioned by them, so as to leave no room for hesitation in its acceptance.

Nor need it be thought that, because the ultimate methods of work employed by painters vary according to the particular effects produced by each, there would be any difficulty in obtaining their collective assent to a system of elementary precept. The facts of which it is necessary that the student should be assured in his early efforts, are so simple, so few, and so well known to all able draughtsmen that, as I have just said, it would be rather doubt of the need of stating what seemed to them self-evident, than reluctance to speak authoritatively on points capable of dispute, that would stand in the way of their giving form to a code of general instruction. To take merely two instances: It will perhaps appear hardly credible that among amateur students, however far advanced in more showy accomplishments, there will not be found one in a hundred who can make an accurate drawing to scale. It is much if they can copy anything with approximate fidelity of its real size. Now, the inaccuracy of eye which prevents a student from drawing to scale is in fact nothing else than an entire want of appreciation of proportion, and therefore of composition. He who alters the relations of dimensions to each other in his copy, shows that he does not enjoy those relations in the original--that is to say, that all appreciation of noble design (which is based on the most exquisite relations of magnitude) is impossible to him. To give him habits of mathematical accuracy in transference of the outline of complex form, is therefore among the first, and even among the most important, means of educating his taste. A student who can fix with precision the cardinal points of a bird's wing, extended in any fixed position, and can then draw the curves of its individual plumes without measurable error, has advanced further towards a power of understanding the design of the great masters than he could by reading many volumes of criticism, or passing many months in undisciplined examination of works of art.

161. Again, it will be found that among amateur students there is almost uni-

versal deficiency in the power of expressing the roundness of a surface. They frequently draw with considerable dexterity and vigour, but never attain the slightest sense of those modulations in form which can only be expressed by gradations in shade. They leave sharp edges to their blots of colour, sharp angles in their contours of lines, and conceal from themselves their incapacity of completion by redundance of object. The assurance to such persons that no object could be rightly seen or drawn until the draughtsman had acquired the power of modulating surfaces by gradations wrought with some pointed instrument (whether pen, pencil, or chalk), would at once prevent much vain labour, and put an end to many errors of that worst kind which not only retard the student, but blind him; which prevent him from either attaining excellence himself, or understanding it in others.

162. It would be easy, did time admit it, to give instances of other principles which it is equally essential that the student should know, and certain that all painters of eminence would sanction; while even those respecting which some doubt may exist in their application to consummate practice, are yet perfectly determinable, so far as they are needed to guide a beginner. It may, for instance, be a question how far local colour should be treated as an element of chiaroscuro in a master's drawing of the human form. But there can be no question that it must be so treated in a boy's study of a tulip or a trout.

163. A still more important point would be gained if authoritative testimony of the same kind could be given to the merit and exclusive sufficiency of any series of examples of works of art, such as could at once be put within the reach of masters of schools. For the modern student labours under heavy disadvantages in what at first sight might appear an assistance to him, namely, the number of examples of many different styles which surround him in galleries or museums. His mind is disturbed by the inconsistencies of various excellences, and by his own predilection for false beauties in second or third-rate works. He is thus prevented from observing any one example long enough to understand its merit, or following any one method long enough to obtain facility in its practice. It seems, therefore, very desirable that some such standard of art should be fixed for all our schools,--a standard which, it must be remembered, need not necessarily be the highest possible, provided only it is the rightest possible. It is not to be hoped that the student should imitate works of the most exalted merit, but much to be desired that he should be guided by those

which have fewest faults.

164. Perhaps, therefore, the most serviceable examples which could be set before youth might be found in the studies or drawings, rather than in the pictures, of first-rate masters; and the art of photography enables us to put renderings of such studies, which for most practical purposes are as good as the originals, on the walls of every school in the kingdom. Supposing (I merely name these as examples of what I mean), the standard of manner in light-and-shade drawing fixed by Leonardo's study, No. 19, in the collection of photographs lately published from drawings in the Florence Gallery; the standard of pen drawing with a wash, fixed by Titian's sketch, No. 30 in the same collection; that of etching, fixed by Rembrandt's spotted shell; and that of point work with the pure line, by Duerer's crest with the cock; every effort of the pupil, whatever the instrument in his hand, would infallibly tend in a right direction, and the perception of the merits of these four works, or of any others like them, once attained thoroughly, by efforts, however distant or despairing, to copy portions of them, would lead securely in due time to the appreciation of other modes of excellence.

165. I cannot, of course, within the limits of this paper, proceed to any statement of the present requirements of the English operative as regards art education. But I do not regret this, for it seems to me very desirable that our attention should for the present be concentrated on the more immediate object of general instruction. Whatever the public demand the artist will soon produce; and the best education which the operative can receive is the refusal of bad work and the acknowledgment of good. There is no want of genius among us, still less of industry. The least that we do is laborious, and the worst is wonderful. But there is a want among us, deep and wide, of discretion in directing toil, and of delight in being led by imagination. In past time, though the masses of the nation were less informed than they are now, they were for that very reason simpler judges and happier gazers; it must be ours to substitute the gracious sympathy of the understanding for the bright gratitude of innocence. An artist can always paint well for those who are lightly pleased or wisely displeased, but he cannot paint for those who are dull in applause and false in condemnation.

REMARKS ADDRESSED

TO THE MANSFIELD ART NIGHT CLASS

Oct. 14th, 1873.[22]

166. It is to be remembered that the giving of prizes can only be justified on the ground of their being the reward of superior diligence and more obedient attention to the directions of the teacher. They must never be supposed, because practically they never can become, indications of superior genius; unless in so far as genius is likely to be diligent and obedient, beyond the strength and temper of the dull.

[Note 22: This address was written for the Art Night Class, Mansfield, but not delivered by me. In my absence--I forget from what cause, but inevitable--the Duke of St. Albans honoured me by reading it to the meeting.]

But it so frequently happens that the stimulus of vanity, acting on minds of inferior calibre, produces for a time an industry surpassing the tranquil and self-possessed exertion of real power, that it may be questioned whether the custom of bestowing prizes at all may not ultimately cease in our higher Schools of Art, unless in the form of substantial assistance given to deserving students who stand in need of it: a kind of prize, the claim to which, in its nature, would depend more on accidental circumstances, and generally good conduct, than on genius.

167. But, without any reference to the opinion of others, and without any chance of partiality in your own, there is one test by which you can all determine the rate of your real progress.

Examine, after every period of renewed industry, how far you have enlarged your faculty of *admiration*.

Consider how much more you can see, to reverence, in the work of masters; and how much more to love, in the work of nature.

This is the only constant and infallible test of progress. That you wonder more at the work of great men, and that you care more for natural objects.

You have often been told by your teachers to expect this last result: but I fear that the tendency of modern thought is to reject the idea of that essential difference in rank between one intellect and another, of which increasing reverence is the wise acknowledgment.

You may, at least in early years, test accurately your power of doing anything in the least rightly, by your increasing conviction that you never will be able to do it as well as it has been done by others.

168. That is a lesson, I repeat, which differs much, I fear, from the one you are commonly taught. The vulgar and incomparably false saying of Macaulay's, that the intellectual giants of one age become the intellectual pigmies of the next, has been the text of too many sermons lately preached to you.

You think you are going to do better things--each of you--than Titian and Phidias--write better than Virgil--think more wisely than Solomon.

My good young people, this is the foolishest, quite pre-eminently--perhaps almost the harmfullest--notion that could possibly be put into your empty little eggshells of heads. There is not one in a million of you who can ever be great in *any* thing. To be greater than the greatest that *have* been, is permitted perhaps to one man in Europe in the course of two or three centuries. But because you cannot be Handel and Mozart--is it any reason why you should not learn to sing "God save the Queen" properly, when you have a mind to? Because a girl cannot be prima donna in the Italian Opera, is it any reason that she should not learn to play a jig for her brothers and sisters in good time, or a soft little tune for her tired mother, or that she should not sing to please herself, among the dew, on a May morning? Believe me, joy, humility, and usefulness, always go together: as insolence with misery, and these both with destructiveness. You may learn with proud teachers how to throw down the Vendome Column, and burn the Louvre, but never how to lay so much as one touch of safe colour, or one layer of steady stone: and if indeed there be among you a youth of true genius, be assured that he will distinguish himself first, not by petulance or by disdain, but by discerning firmly what to admire, and whom to obey.

169. It will, I hope, be the result of the interest lately awakened in art through our provinces, to enable each town of importance to obtain, in permanent possession, a few--and it is desirable there should be no more than a few--examples of consummate and masterful art: an engraving or two by Duerer--a single portrait

by Reynolds--a fifteenth century Florentine drawing--a thirteenth century French piece of painted glass, and the like; and that, in every town occupied in a given manufacture, examples of unquestionable excellence in that manufacture should be made easily accessible in its civic museum.

I must ask you, however, to observe very carefully that I use the word ***manufacture*** in its literal and proper sense. It means the making of things ***by the hand***. It does not mean the making them by machinery. And, while I plead with you for a true humility in rivalship with the works of others, I plead with you also for a just pride in what you really can honestly do yourself.

You must neither think your work the best ever done by man:--nor, on the other hand, think that the tongs and poker can do better--and that, although you are wiser than Solomon, all this wisdom of yours can be outshone by a shovelful of coke.

170. Let me take, for instance, the manufacture of lace, for which, I believe, your neighbouring town of Nottingham enjoys renown. There is still some distinction between machine-made and hand-made lace. I will suppose that distinction so far done away with, that, a pattern once invented, you can spin lace as fast as you now do thread. Everybody then might wear, not only lace collars, but lace gowns. Do you think they would be more comfortable in them than they are now in plain stuff--or that, when everybody could wear them, anybody would be proud of wearing them? A spider may perhaps be rationally proud of his own cobweb, even though all the fields in the morning are covered with the like, for he made it himself--but suppose a machine spun it for him?

Suppose all the gossamer were Nottingham-made, would a sensible spider be either prouder, or happier, think you?

A sensible spider! You cannot perhaps imagine such a creature. Yet surely a spider is clever enough for his own ends?

You think him an insensible spider, only because he cannot understand yours--and is apt to impede yours. Well, be assured of this, sense in human creatures is shown also, not by cleverness in promoting their own ends and interests, but by quickness in understanding other people's ends and interests, and by putting our own work and keeping our own wishes in harmony with theirs.

171. But I return to my point, of cheapness. You don't think that it would be

convenient, or even creditable, for women to wash the doorsteps or dish the dinners in lace gowns? Nay, even for the most ladylike occupations--reading, or writing, or playing with her children--do you think a lace gown, or even a lace collar, so great an advantage or dignity to a woman? If you think of it, you will find the whole value of lace, as a possession, depends on the fact of its having a beauty which has been the reward of industry and attention.

That the thing itself is a prize--a thing which everybody cannot have. That it proves, by the ***look*** of it, the ***ability*** of its ***maker***; that it proves, by the ***rarity*** of it, the ***dignity*** of its ***wearer***--either that she has been so industrious as to save money, which can buy, say, a piece of jewellery, of gold tissue, or of fine lace--or else, that she is a noble person, to whom her neighbours concede, as an honour, the privilege of wearing finer dresses than they.

If they all choose to have lace too--if it ceases to be a prize--it becomes, does it not, only a cobweb?

The real good of a piece of lace, then, you will find, is that it should show, first, that the designer of it had a pretty fancy; next, that the maker of it had fine fingers; lastly, that the wearer of it has worthiness or dignity enough to obtain what is difficult to obtain, and common sense enough not to wear it on all occasions. I limit myself, in what farther I have to say, to the question of the manufacture--nay, of one requisite in the manufacture: that which I have just called a pretty fancy.

172. What do you suppose I mean by a pretty fancy? Do you think that, by learning to draw, and looking at flowers, you will ever get the ability to design a piece of lace beautifully? By no means. If that were so, everybody would soon learn to draw--everybody would design lace prettily--and then,--nobody would be paid for designing it. To some extent, that will indeed be the result of modern endeavour to teach design. But against all such endeavours, mother-wit, in the end, will hold her own.

But anybody who ***has*** this mother-wit, may make the exercise of it more pleasant to themselves, and more useful to other people, by learning to draw.

An Indian worker in gold, or a Scandinavian worker in iron, or an old French worker in thread, could produce indeed beautiful design out of nothing but groups of knots and spirals: but you, when you are rightly educated, may render your knots and spirals infinitely more interesting by making them suggestive of natural forms, and rich in elements of true knowledge.

173. You know, for instance, the pattern which for centuries has been the basis of ornament in Indian shawls--the bulging leaf ending in a spiral. The Indian produces beautiful designs with nothing but that spiral. You cannot better his powers of design, but you may make them more civil and useful by adding knowledge of nature to invention.

Suppose you learn to draw rightly, and, therefore, to know correctly the spirals of springing ferns--not that you may give ugly names to all the species of them--but that you may understand the grace and vitality of every hour of their existence. Suppose you have sense and cleverness enough to translate the essential character of this beauty into forms expressible by simple lines--therefore expressible by thread--you might then have a series of fern-patterns which would each contain points of distinctive interest and beauty, and of scientific truth, and yet be variable by fancy, with quite as much ease as the meaningless Indian one. Similarly, there is no form of leaf, of flower, or of insect, which might not become suggestive to you, and expressible in terms of manufacture, so as to be interesting, and useful to others.

174. Only don't think that this kind of study will ever "pay" in the vulgar sense.

It will make you wiser and happier. But do you suppose that it is the law of God, or nature, that people shall be paid in money for becoming wiser and happier? They are so, by that law, for honest work; and as all honest work makes people wiser and happier, they are indeed, in some sort, paid in money for becoming wise.

But if you seek wisdom only that you may get money, believe me, you are exactly on the foolishest of all fools' errands. "She is more precious than rubies"--but do you think that is only because she will help you to buy rubies?

"All the things thou canst desire are not to be compared to her." Do you think that is only because she will enable you to get all the things you desire? She is offered to you as a blessing *in herself*. She is the reward of kindness, of modesty, of industry. She is the prize of Prizes--and alike in poverty or in riches--the strength of your Life now, the earnest of whatever Life is to come.

SOCIAL POLICY

BASED ON NATURAL SELECTION.

Paper read before the Metaphysical Society, May 11th, 1875.[23]

175. It has always seemed to me that Societies like this of ours, happy in including members not a little diverse in thought and various in knowledge, might be more useful to the public than perhaps they can fairly be said to have approved themselves hitherto, by using their variety of power rather to support intellectual conclusions by concentric props, than to shake them with rotatory storms of wit; and modestly endeavouring to initiate the building of walls for the Bridal city of Science, in which no man will care to identify the particular stones he lays, rather than complying farther with the existing picturesque, but wasteful, practice of every knight to throw up a feudal tower of his own opinions, tenable only by the most active pugnacity, and pierced rather with arrow-slits from which to annoy his neighbours, than windows to admit light or air.

> [Note 23: I trust that the Society will not consider its privileges violated by the publication of an essay, which, for such audience, I wrote with more than ordinary care.]

176. The paper read at our last meeting was unquestionably, within the limits its writer had prescribed to himself, so logically sound, that (encouraged also by the suggestion of some of our most influential members), I shall endeavour to make the matter of our to-night's debate consequent upon it, and suggestive of possibly further advantageous deductions.

It will be remembered that, in reference to the statement in the Bishop of Peterborough's Paper, of the moral indifference of certain courses of conduct on the postulate of the existence only of a Mechanical base of Morals, it was observed by Dr. Adam Clarke that, even on such mechanical basis, the word "moral" might still be applied specially to any course of action which tended to the development of the human race. Whereupon I ventured myself to inquire, in what direction such development was to be understood as taking place; and the discussion of this point being then dropped for want of time, I would ask the Society's permission to bring it again before them this evening in a somewhat more extended form; for in reality the question respecting the development of men is twofold,--first, namely, in what direction; and secondly, in what social relations, it is to be sought.

I would therefore at present ask more deliberately than I could at our last meeting,--first, in what direction it is desirable that the development of humanity should take place? Should it, for instance, as in Greece, be of physical beauty,-

-emulation, (Hesiod's second Eris),--pugnacity, and patriotism? or, as in modern England, of physical ugliness,--envy, (Hesiod's first Eris),--cowardice, and selfishness? or, as by a conceivably humane but hitherto unexampled education might be attempted, of physical beauty, humility, courage, and affection, which should make all the world one native land, and [Greek: pasa ge taphos]?

177. I do not doubt but that the first automatic impulse of all our automatic friends here present, on hearing this sentence, will be strenuously to deny the accuracy of my definition of the aims of modern English education. Without attempting to defend it, I would only observe that this automatic development of solar caloric in scientific minds must be grounded on an automatic sensation of injustice done to the members of the School Board, as well as to many other automatically well-meaning and ingenious persons; and that this sense of the injuriousness and offensiveness of my definition cannot possibly have any other basis (if I may be permitted to continue my professional similitudes) than the fallen remnants and goodly stones, not one now left on another, but still forming an unremovable cumulus of ruin, and eternal Birs Nimroud, as it were, on the site of the old belfry of Christian morality, whose top looked once so like touching Heaven.

For no offence could be taken at my definition, unless traceable to adamantine conviction,--that ugliness, however indefinable, envy, however natural, and cowardice, however commercially profitable, are nevertheless eternally disgraceful; contrary, that is to say, to the grace of our Lord Christ, if there be among us any Christ; to the grace of the King's Majesty, if there be among us any King; and to the grace even of Christless and Kingless Manhood, if there be among us any Manhood.

To this fixed conception of a difference between Better and Worse, or, when carried to the extreme, between good and evil in conduct, we all, it seems to me, instinctively and, therefore, rightly, attach the term of Moral sense;--the sense, for instance, that it would be better if the members of this Society who are usually automatically absent were, instead, automatically present; or better, that this Paper, if (which is, perhaps, too likely) it be thought automatically impertinent, had been made by the molecular action of my cerebral particles, pertinent.

178. Trusting, therefore, without more ado, to the strength of rampart in this Old Sarum of the Moral sense, however subdued into vague banks under the mod-

ern steam-plough, I will venture to suppose the first of my two questions to have been answered by the choice on the part at least of a majority of our Council, of the third direction of development above specified as being the properly called "moral" one; and will go on to the second subject of inquiry, both more difficult and of great practical importance in the political crisis through which Europe is passing,-- namely, what relations between men are to be desired, or with resignation allowed, in the course of their Moral Development?

Whether, that is to say, we should try to make some men beautiful at the cost of ugliness in others, and some men virtuous at the cost of vice in others,--or rather, all men beautiful and virtuous in the degree possible to each under a system of equitable education? And evidently our first business is to consider in what terms the choice is put to us by Nature. What can we do, if we would? What must we do, whether we will or not? How high can we raise the level of a diffused Learning and Morality? and how far shall we be compelled, if we limit, to exaggerate, the advantages and injuries of our system? And are we prepared, if the extremity be inevitable, to push to their utmost the relations implied when we take off our hats to each other, and triple the tiara of the Saint in Heaven, while we leave the sinner bareheaded in Cocytus?

179. It is well, perhaps, that I should at once confess myself to hold the principle of limitation in its utmost extent; and to entertain no doubt of the rightness of my ideal, but only of its feasibility. I am ill at ease, for instance, in my uncertainty whether our greatly regretted Chairman will ever be Pope, or whether some people whom I could mention, (not, of course, members of our Society,) will ever be in Cocytus.

But there is no need, if we would be candid, to debate the principle in these violences of operation, any more than the proper methods of distributing food, on the supposition that the difference between a Paris dinner and a platter of Scotch porridge must imply that one-half of mankind are to die of eating, and the rest of having nothing to eat. I will therefore take for example a case in which the discrimination is less conclusive.

180. When I stop writing metaphysics this morning it will be to arrange some drawings for a young lady to copy. They are leaves of the best illuminated MSS. I have, and I am going to spend my whole afternoon in explaining to her what she is

to aim at in copying them.

Now, I would not lend these leaves to any other young lady that I know of; nor give up my afternoon to, perhaps, more than two or three other young ladies that I know of. But to keep to the first-instanced one, I lend her my books, and give her, for what they are worth, my time and most careful teaching, because she at present paints butterflies better than any other girl I know, and has a peculiar capacity for the softening of plumes and finessing of antennae. Grant me to be a good teacher, and grant her disposition to be such as I suppose, and the result will be what might at first appear an indefensible iniquity, namely, that this girl, who has already excellent gifts, having also excellent teaching, will become perhaps the best butterfly-painter in England; while myriads of other girls, having originally inferior powers, and attracting no attention from the Slade Professor, will utterly lose their at present cultivable faculties of entomological art, and sink into the vulgar career of wives and mothers, to which we have Mr. Mill's authority for holding it a grievous injustice that any girl should be irrevocably condemned.

181. There is no need that I should be careful in enumerating the various modes, analogous to this, in which the Natural selection of which we have lately heard, perhaps, somewhat more than enough, provokes and approves the Professorial selection which I am so bold as to defend; and if the automatic instincts of equity in us, which revolt against the great ordinance of Nature and practice of Man, that "to him that hath, shall more be given," are to be listened to when the possessions in question are only of wisdom and virtue, let them at least prove their sincerity by correcting, first, the injustice which has established itself respecting more tangible and more esteemed property; and terminating the singular arrangement prevalent in commercial Europe that to every man with a hundred pounds in his pocket there shall annually be given three, to every man with a thousand, thirty, and to every man with nothing, none.

182. I am content here to leave under the scrutiny of the evening my general statement, that as human development, when moral, is with special effort in a given direction, so, when moral, it is with special effort in favour of a limited class; but I yet trespass for a few moments on your patience in order to note that the acceptance of this second principle still leaves it debatable to what point the disfavour of the reprobate class, or the privileges of the elect, may advisably extend. For I cannot

but feel for my own part as if the daily bread of moral instruction might at least be so widely broken among the multitude as to preserve them from utter destitution and pauperism in virtue; and that even the simplest and lowest of the rabble should not be so absolutely sons of perdition, but that each might say for himself,--"For my part--no offence to the General, or any man of quality--I hope to be saved." Whereas it is, on the contrary, implied by the habitual expressions of the wisest aristocrats, that the completely developed persons whose Justice and Fortitude--poles to the Cardinal points of virtue--are marked as their sufficient characteristics by the great Roman moralist in his phrase, "Justus, et tenax propositi," will in the course of nature be opposed by a civic ardour, not merely of the innocent and ignorant, but of persons developed in a contrary direction to that which I have ventured to call "moral," and therefore not merely incapable of desiring or applauding what is right, but in an evil harmony, ***prava jubentium***, clamorously demanding what is wrong.

183. The point to which both Natural and Divine Selection would permit us to advance in severity towards this profane class, to which the enduring "Ecce Homo," or manifestation of any properly human sentiment or person, must always be instinctively abominable, seems to be conclusively indicated by the order following on the parable of the Talents,--"Those mine enemies, bring hither, and slay them before me." Nor does it seem reasonable, on the other hand, to set the limits of favouritism more narrowly. For even if, among fallible mortals, there may frequently be ground for the hesitation of just men to award the punishment of death to their enemies, the most beautiful story, to my present knowledge, of all antiquity, that of Cleobis and Bito, might suggest to them the fitness on some occasions, of distributing without any hesitation the reward of death to their friends. For surely the logical conclusion of the Bishop of Peterborough, respecting the treatment due to old women who have nothing supernatural about them, holds with still greater force when applied to the case of old women who have everything supernatural about them; and while it might remain questionable to some of us whether we had any right to deprive an invalid who had no soul, of what might still remain to her of even painful earthly existence; it would surely on the most religious grounds be both our privilege and our duty at once to dismiss any troublesome sufferer who ***had*** a soul, to the distant and inoffensive felicities of heaven.

184. But I believe my hearers will approve me in again declining to disturb the serene confidence of daily action by these speculations in extreme; the really useful conclusion which, it seems to me, cannot be evaded, is that, without going so far as the exile of the inconveniently wicked, and translation of the inconveniently sick, to their proper spiritual mansions, we should at least be certain that we do not waste care in protracting disease which might have been spent in preserving health; that we do not appease in the splendour of our turreted hospitals the feelings of compassion which, rightly directed, might have prevented the need of them; nor pride ourselves on the peculiar form of Christian benevolence which leaves the cottage roofless to model the prison, and spends itself with zealous preference where, in the keen words of Carlyle, if you desire the material on which maximum expenditure of means and effort will produce the minimum result, "here you accurately have it."

185. I cannot but, in conclusion, most respectfully but most earnestly, express my hope that measures may be soon taken by the Lords Spiritual of England to assure her doubting mind of the real existence of that supernatural revelation of the basis of morals to which the Bishop of Peterborough referred in the close of his paper; or at least to explain to her bewildered populace the real meaning and force of the Ten Commandments, whether written originally by the finger of God or Man. To me personally, I own, as one of that bewildered populace, that the essay by one of our most distinguished members on the Creed of Christendom seems to stand in need of explicit answer from our Divines; but if not, and the common application of the terms "Word of God" to the books of Scripture be against all question tenable, it becomes yet more imperative on the interpreters of that Scripture to see that they are not made void by our traditions, and that the Mortal sins of Covetousness, Fraud, Usury, and contention be not the essence of a National life orally professing submission to the laws of Christ, and satisfaction in His Love.

J. RUSKIN.

"Thou shalt not covet; but tradition Approves all forms of Competition."

ARTHUR CLOUGH.

The Codes Of Hammurabi And Moses
W. W. Davies

The discovery of the Hammurabi Code is one of the greatest achievements of archaeology, and is of paramount interest, not only to the student of the Bible, but also to all those interested in ancient history...

Religion   **ISBN:** *1-59462-338-4*

QTY

Pages:132
MSRP $12.95

The Theory of Moral Sentiments
Adam Smith

This work from 1749. contains original theories of conscience amd moral judgment and it is the foundation for systemof morals.

Philosophy **ISBN:** *1-59462-777-0*

QTY

Pages:536
MSRP $19.95

Jessica's First Prayer
Hesba Stretton

In a screened and secluded corner of one of the many railway-bridges which span the streets of London there could be seen a few years ago, from five o'clock every morning until half past eight, a tidily set-out coffee-stall, consisting of a trestle and board, upon which stood two large tin cans, with a small fire of charcoal burning under each so as to keep the coffee boiling during the early hours of the morning when the work-people were thronging into the city on their way to their daily toil...

Childrens   **ISBN:** *1-59462-373-2*

QTY

Pages:84
MSRP $9.95

My Life and Work
Henry Ford

Henry Ford revolutionized the world with his implementation of mass production for the Model T automobile. Gain valuable business insight into his life and work with his own auto-biography... "We have only started on our development of our country we have not as yet, with all our talk of wonderful progress, done more than scratch the surface. The progress has been wonderful enough but..."

Biographies/   **ISBN:** *1-59462-198-5*

QTY

Pages:300
MSRP $21.95

The Art of Cross-Examination
Francis Wellman

QTY

I presume it is the experience of every author, after his first book is published upon an important subject, to be almost overwhelmed with a wealth of ideas and illustrations which could readily have been included in his book, and which to his own mind, at least, seem to make a second edition inevitable. Such certainly was the case with me; and when the first edition had reached its sixth impression in five months, I rejoiced to learn that it seemed to my publishers that the book had met with a sufficiently favorable reception to justify a second and considerably enlarged edition. ..

Pages:412

Reference   ISBN: *1-59462-647-2*   *MSRP $19.95*

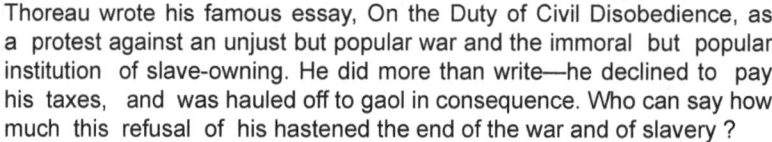

On the Duty of Civil Disobedience
Henry David Thoreau

QTY

Thoreau wrote his famous essay, On the Duty of Civil Disobedience, as a protest against an unjust but popular war and the immoral but popular institution of slave-owning. He did more than write—he declined to pay his taxes, and was hauled off to gaol in consequence. Who can say how much this refusal of his hastened the end of the war and of slavery ?

Pages:48

Law   ISBN: *1-59462-747-9*   *MSRP $7.45*

Dream Psychology Psychoanalysis for Beginners
Sigmund Freud

QTY

Sigmund Freud, born Sigismund Schlomo Freud (May 6, 1856 - September 23, 1939), was a Jewish-Austrian neurologist and psychiatrist who co-founded the psychoanalytic school of psychology. Freud is best known for his theories of the unconscious mind, especially involving the mechanism of repression; his redefinition of sexual desire as mobile and directed towards a wide variety of objects; and his therapeutic techniques, especially his understanding of transference in the therapeutic relationship and the presumed value of dreams as sources of insight into unconscious desires.

Pages:196

Psychology   ISBN: *1-59462-905-6*   *MSRP $15.45*

The Miracle of Right Thought
Orison Swett Marden

QTY

Believe with all of your heart that you will do what you were made to do. When the mind has once formed the habit of holding cheerful, happy, prosperous pictures, it will not be easy to form the opposite habit. It does not matter how improbable or how far away this realization may see, or how dark the prospects may be, if we visualize them as best we can, as vividly as possible, hold tenaciously to them and vigorously struggle to attain them, they will gradually become actualized, realized in the life. But a desire, a longing without endeavor, a yearning abandoned or held indifferently will vanish without realization.

Pages:360

Self Help   ISBN: *1-59462-644-8*   *MSRP $25.45*

QTY

The Rosicrucian Cosmo-Conception Mystic Christianity *by Max Heindel*   ISBN: *1-59462-188-8*   **$38.95**
The Rosicrucian Cosmo-conception is not dogmatic, neither does it appeal to any other authority than the reason of the student. It is: not controversial, but is: sent forth in the, hope that it may help to clear...   *New Age/Religion Pages 646*

Abandonment To Divine Providence *by Jean-Pierre de Caussade*   ISBN: *1-59462-228-0*   **$25.95**
"The Rev. Jean Pierre de Caussade was one of the most remarkable spiritual writers of the Society of Jesus in France in the 18th Century. His death took place at Toulouse in 1751. His works have gone through many editions and have been republished...   *Inspirational/Religion Pages 400*

Mental Chemistry *by Charles Haanel*   ISBN: *1-59462-192-6*   **$23.95**
Mental Chemistry allows the change of material conditions by combining and appropriately utilizing the power of the mind. Much like applied chemistry creates something new and unique out of careful combinations of chemicals the mastery of mental chemistry...   *New Age Pages 354*

The Letters of Robert Browning and Elizabeth Barret Barrett 1845-1846 vol II   ISBN: *1-59462-193-4*   **$35.95**
by Robert Browning and Elizabeth Barrett   *Biographies Pages 596*

Gleanings In Genesis (volume I) *by Arthur W. Pink*   ISBN: *1-59462-130-6*   **$27.45**
Appropriately has Genesis been termed "the seed plot of the Bible" for in it we have, in germ form, almost all of the great doctrines which are afterwards fully developed in the books of Scripture which follow...   *Religion/Inspirational Pages 420*

The Master Key *by L. W. de Laurence*   ISBN: *1-59462-001-6*   **$30.95**
In no branch of human knowledge has there been a more lively increase of the spirit of research during the past few years than in the study of Psychology, Concentration and Mental Discipline. The requests for authentic lessons in Thought Control, Mental Discipline and...   *New Age/Business Pages 422*

The Lesser Key Of Solomon Goetia *by L. W. de Laurence*   ISBN: *1-59462-092-X*   **$9.95**
This translation of the first book of the "Lernegton" which is now for the first time made accessible to students of Talismanic Magic was done, after careful collation and edition, from numerous Ancient Manuscripts in Hebrew, Latin, and French...   *New Age/Occult Pages 92*

Rubaiyat Of Omar Khayyam *by Edward Fitzgerald*   ISBN: *1-59462-332-5*   **$13.95**
Edward Fitzgerald, whom the world has already learned, in spite of his own efforts to remain within the shadow of anonymity, to look upon as one of the rarest poets of the century, was born at Bredfield, in Suffolk, on the 31st of March, 1809. He was the third son of John Purcell...   *Music Pages 172*

Ancient Law *by Henry Maine*   ISBN: *1-59462-128-4*   **$29.95**
The chief object of the following pages is to indicate some of the earliest ideas of mankind, as they are reflected in Ancient Law, and to point out the relation of those ideas to modern thought.   *Religion/History Pages 452*

Far-Away Stories *by William J. Locke*   ISBN: *1-59462-129-2*   **$19.45**
"Good wine needs no bush, but a collection of mixed vintages does. And this book is just such a collection. Some of the stories I do not want to remain buried for ever in the museum files of dead magazine-numbers an author's not unpardonable vanity..."   *Fiction Pages 272*

Life of David Crockett *by David Crockett*   ISBN: *1-59462-250-7*   **$27.45**
"Colonel David Crockett was one of the most remarkable men of the times in which he lived. Born in humble life, but gifted with a strong will, an indomitable courage, and unremitting perseverance...   *Biographies/New Age Pages 424*

Lip-Reading *by Edward Nitchie*   ISBN: *1-59462-206-X*   **$25.95**
Edward B. Nitchie, founder of the New York School for the Hard of Hearing, now the Nitchie School of Lip-Reading, Inc, wrote "LIP-READING Principles and Practice". The development and perfecting of this meritorious work on lip-reading was an undertaking...   *How-to Pages 400*

A Handbook of Suggestive Therapeutics, Applied Hypnotism, Psychic Science   ISBN: *1-59462-214-0*   **$24.95**
by Henry Munro   *Health/New Age/Health/Self-help Pages 376*

A Doll's House: and Two Other Plays *by Henrik Ibsen*   ISBN: *1-59462-112-8*   **$19.95**
Henrik Ibsen created this classic when in revolutionary 1848 Rome. Introducing some striking concepts in playwriting for the realist genre, this play has been studied the world over.   *Fiction/Classics/Plays 308*

The Light of Asia *by sir Edwin Arnold*   ISBN: *1-59462-204-3*   **$13.95**
In this poetic masterpiece, Edwin Arnold describes the life and teachings of Buddha. The man who was to become known as Buddha to the world was born as Prince Gautama of India but he rejected the worldly riches and abandoned the reigns of power when... Religion/History/Biographies Pages 170

The Complete Works of Guy de Maupassant *by Guy de Maupassant*   ISBN: *1-59462-157-8*   **$16.95**
"For days and days, nights and nights, I had dreamed of that first kiss which was to consecrate our engagement, and I knew not on what spot I should put my lips..."   *Fiction/Classics Pages 240*

The Art of Cross-Examination *by Francis L. Wellman*   ISBN: *1-59462-309-0*   **$26.95**
Written by a renowned trial lawyer, Wellman imparts his experience and uses case studies to explain how to use psychology to extract desired information through questioning.   *How-to/Science/Reference Pages 408*

Answered or Unanswered? *by Louisa Vaughan*   ISBN: *1-59462-248-5*   **$10.95**
Miracles of Faith in China   *Religion Pages 112*

The Edinburgh Lectures on Mental Science (1909) *by Thomas*   ISBN: *1-59462-008-3*   **$11.95**
This book contains the substance of a course of lectures recently given by the writer in the Queen Street Hall, Edinburgh. Its purpose is to indicate the Natural Principles governing the relation between Mental Action and Material Conditions...   *New Age/Psychology Pages 148*

Ayesha *by H. Rider Haggard*   ISBN: *1-59462-301-5*   **$24.95**
Verily and indeed it is the unexpected that happens! Probably if there was one person upon the earth from whom the Editor of this, and of a certain previous history, did not expect to hear again...   *Classics Pages 380*

Ayala's Angel *by Anthony Trollope*   ISBN: *1-59462-352-X*   **$29.95**
The two girls were both pretty, but Lucy who was twenty-one who supposed to be simple and comparatively unattractive, whereas Ayala was credited, as her Bombwhat romantic name might show, with poetic charm and a taste for romance. Ayala when her father died was nineteen...   Fiction Pages 484

The American Commonwealth *by James Bryce*   ISBN: *1-59462-286-8*   **$34.45**
An interpretation of American democratic political theory. It examines political mechanics and society from the perspective of Scotsman James Bryce   *Politics Pages 572*

Stories of the Pilgrims *by Margaret P. Pumphrey*   ISBN: *1-59462-116-0*   **$17.95**
This book explores pilgrims religious oppression in England as well as their escape to Holland and eventual crossing to America on the Mayflower, and their early days in New England...   *History Pages 268*

QTY

The Fasting Cure *by Sinclair Upton*   ISBN: *1-59462-222-1*   **$13.95**
In the Cosmopolitan Magazine for May, 1910, and in the Contemporary Review (London) for April, 1910, I published an article dealing with my experiences in fasting. I have written a great many magazine articles, but never one which attracted so much attention... New Age/Self Help/Health Pages 164

Hebrew Astrology *by Sepharial*   ISBN: *1-59462-308-2*   **$13.45**
In these days of advanced thinking it is a matter of common observation that we have left many of the old landmarks behind and that we are now pressing forward to greater heights and to a wider horizon than that which represented the mind-content of our progenitors... Astrology Pages 144

Thought Vibration or The Law of Attraction in the Thought World   ISBN: *1-59462-127-6*   **$12.95**
by William Walker Atkinson   Psychology/Religion Pages 144

Optimism *by Helen Keller*   ISBN: *1-59462-108-X*   **$15.95**
Helen Keller was blind, deaf, and mute since 19 months old, yet famously learned how to overcome these handicaps, communicate with the world, and spread her lectures promoting optimism. An inspiring read for everyone... Biographies/Inspirational Pages 84

Sara Crewe *by Frances Burnett*   ISBN: *1-59462-360-0*   **$9.45**
In the first place, Miss Minchin lived in London. Her home was a large, dull, tall one, in a large, dull square, where all the houses were alike, and all the sparrows were alike, and where all the door-knockers made the same heavy sound... Childrens/Classic Pages 88

The Autobiography of Benjamin Franklin *by Benjamin Franklin*   ISBN: *1-59462-135-7*   **$24.95**
The Autobiography of Benjamin Franklin has probably been more extensively read than any other American historical work, and no other book of its kind has had such ups and downs of fortune. Franklin lived for many years in England, where he was agent... Biographies/History Pages 332

Name	
Email	
Telephone	
Address	
City, State ZIP	

☐ **Credit Card**   ☐ **Check / Money Order**

Credit Card Number	
Expiration Date	
Signature	

Please Mail to: Book Jungle
PO Box 2226
Champaign, IL 61825
or Fax to: 630-214-0564

www.ingramcontent.com/pod-product-compliance
Lightning Source LLC
Chambersburg PA
CBHW080747250626
47162CB00010B/3055